Mates, Dates & Portobello Princesses

D0508791

BRON-Y-WENDON

• HOLIDAY PARKS •

NANT-Y-GLYN

Cathy Hopkins is the author of the incredibly successful *Mates, Dates* and *Truth, Dare* books, and has just started a fabulous new series called *Cinnamon Girl*. She lives in North London with her husband and three cats, Molly, Emmylou and Otis.

Cathy spends most of her time locked in a shed at the bottom of the garden pretending to write books but is actually in there listening to music, hippie dancing and talking to her friends on email.

Occasionally she is joined by Molly, the cat who thinks she is a copy-editor and likes to walk all over the keyboard rewriting and deleting any words she doesn't like.

Emmylou and Otis are new to the household. So far they are as insane as the older one. Their favourite game is to run from one side of the house to the other as fast as possible, then see if they can fly if they leap high enough off the furniture. This usually happens at three o'clock in the morning and they land on anyone who happens to be asleep at the time.

Apart from that, Cathy has joined the gym and spends more time than is good for her making up excuses as to why she hasn't got time to go.

Cathy Hopkins

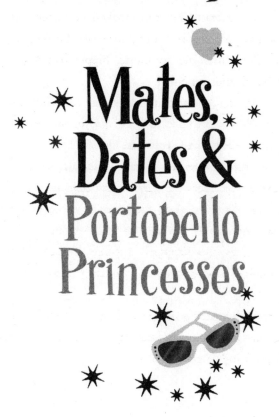

Mates, Dates & Portobello Princesses

PICCADILLY PRESS • LONDON

Big thanks to: Terry Segal for letting me read her teenage diary. I promise I won't reveal details to her mother. Or husband. At least, not yet. To Emma Creighton for the low-down on horse-riding for beginners. To husbando Steve for accompanying me to all the locations in the book in the middle of winter. In the rain. To Brenda and Jude at Piccadilly who are a pleasure to do business with and not forgetting Margot Edwards whose e-mails make my day. Lastly to Rosemary Bromley for saying yes to my books when I was ready to pack it all in and join the Foreign Legion.

First published in Great Britain in 2001
by Piccadilly Press Ltd.,
5 Castle Road, London NW1 8PR

This edition published 2007

Text copyright © Cathy Hopkins, 2001, 2007

All rights reserved. No part of this publication may be
reproduced, stored in a retrieval system, or transmitted in
any form or by any means, electronic, mechanical,
photocopying, recording or otherwise, without the prior
permission of the copyright owner.

The right of Cathy Hopkins to be identified as Author
of this work has been asserted by her in accordance with
the Copyright, Designs and Patents Act 1988

A catalogue record for this book is available from
the British Library

ISBN-13: 978 1 85340 929 5 (trade paperback)

1 3 5 7 9 10 8 6 4 2

Set by Textype Typesetters, Cambridge
Printed in the UK by CPI Bookmarque, Croydon CR0 4TD
Cover design by Simon Davis

Chapter 1

Love Train

'Nesta, is that you?' said Lucy's voice at the other end of the phone. 'You sound weird. Where are you?'

'In the loo, on the train from *hell*,' I groaned.

I could hear her laughing. Why do people always think it's funny when my life turns into total disaster?

'No *seriously*. It's a nightmare. We're stuck in the middle of nowhere. I should have been home hours ago.'

'Sounds like you're in a bucket,' said Lucy. 'The phone's all echoey. Anyway, what are you doing in the loo? You're not stuck in there, are you?' She started laughing again.

'I am in here,' I said primly, 'to talk on my mobile without the whole carriage listening in and hopefully to get some sympathy from someone who's *supposed* to be one of my best friends.'

'I *am* sorry, Nesta. It'll get going again soon.'

'What are you doing?'

'Watching telly. There's a repeat of "The O.C." on. Going to Izzie's later.'

'Lucky thing. I wish I was there. I can't bear this much longer. I'm bored out of my mind.'

'Haven't you got a book with you?'

'Read it.'

'Magazine?'

'Read it.'

'Call Izzie.'

'She's out.'

'Then go and chat to one of the passengers. That'll make the time go faster.'

'Don't even go there. I've got the Family of Satan sitting behind me. Remind me never to have kids.'

'I thought you liked kids?'

'Yeah. But I couldn't eat a whole one. Honestly, it's awful. This little boy behind me is driving me bonkers. Banging on my seat, arguing with his sister, playing some irritating computer game that makes a noise like a police siren. And his parents are just sitting there like he's the most adorable creature ever. I wish they'd tell him to zip it.'

'So move. It's Saturday. Go into weekend first and pay the extra. Have you got enough?'

'Yeah. I moved already. Dad gave me the extra. But because it's Easter, the train's massively overbooked and there aren't enough seats, so they've moved *everyone* into first class. *And* the heating's broken. *And* there's no buffet car! I can't even get a Coke. Stop laughing. I don't see what's so funny.'

'Sorry, Nesta,' said Lucy. 'It's just the thought of you hiding in the loo. You get to go to *all* the trendiest places.'

'Yeah right. Hysterical. Phworr. It smells awful in here; I think someone's been having a sneaky fag. Just a mo, I'm going to spray.'

I got out my CK and squirted into the air. 'That's better. I'm *sooooo* bored, Lucy. Entertain me.'

'Go and sit back down and try some of that meditation we did at school.'

'Oh, gimme a break. That's Izzie's thing.'

'So when will you be back?'

'Dunno. Never by the looks of it. I'm clearly being punished. I've died and gone to hell and am going to be stuck on this train with all these mad people for eternity.'

'You're such a drama queen, Nesta. You'll be back before you know it.'

'I wish. Dad dropped me at Manchester at one o'clock and the journey's supposed to take *three* hours. We've already been on the train that long. And now we appear to have broken down . . . though there've been no announcements to tell us what's going on. What shall I do?'

'Er, I don't know. Put some make-up on.'

'Good idea.' I got out my make-up bag and began to put on some lipstick. 'Oh, hold on a mo,' I said as the train suddenly lurched forward causing me to smear my lippie in a gash up my cheek. 'Oops. I think we're off. Yep. We're moving again . . . Lucy, Lucy . . .?'

My mobile cut out so I checked my appearance in the mirror and gave my hair a quick brush. I wondered if I should spend some more time in there plaiting it. Or maybe I should leave it loose. There was a boy who'd been checking me out the whole journey. He was quite good-looking. People say my hair's one of my best features: it's long right down to my waist. I decided I'd leave it loose. I wanted to look good for when Boy In The Corner made his move. It had to be only a matter of time.

Passengers were staring at me as I made my way back down the carriage. I'm used to it by now as people always look at me. Izzie says it's because I stand out in a crowd as *très* good-looking but sometimes I think it's also because they can't make out where I'm from. I can see their brains are going tick-tick-tick trying to work out what nationality I am. Actually my dad's Italian and my mum's Jamaican. Sometimes I tell people I'm Jamalian or Italaican. That confuses them.

Being hard to identify comes in useful some days though, like when I'm out with Lucy and Izzie and we're in a mad mood. We pretend that we're foreign students. I pretend I'm Spanish or Indian. I could be either. Lucy pretends to be Swedish as she's got blonde hair and high cheekbones and can do a really good accent. And Izzie, for some reason, always pretends to be Norwegian, though with her dark colouring and beautiful eyes she's a typical Irish colleen.

As I squeezed past various irate people sitting in the corridor on their suitcases, an announcement came over the tannoy.

'We apologise for the delay and lack of seats but we are on our way again and will be arriving in Birmingham in a few minutes. However, due to a problem with the engine, we will be stationed there while the engineers rectify it. We will be arriving at Euston approximately two hours later than scheduled.'

A moan went through the train, then a chorus of voices as people got out their mobile phones and began dialling.

'Martha, I'm outside Birmingham. Dunno what time we'll be back. I'll get a taxi.'

'Tom. I'll be late as the train's stuck. I'll call when we're a bit closer.'

'Gina. Damn train's late again. Call you later.'

On and on it went through every carriage.

Then I realised I couldn't find my seat. I checked the other passengers, thinking that maybe I was in the wrong carriage. But no, there was the Family of Satan. Cute Boy

In The Corner. Oh no. Someone was in my seat. An old dear with white hair and glasses. She'd made herself comfortable with a flask of tea and an egg sandwich. I couldn't possibly ask her to move. It would be mean.

I looked around the carriage, but there weren't any other seats. Oh well, I'll just have to stand, I thought. For two and a half hours. Whoopee. Not.

But the gods decided to take pity. A few minutes later, we pulled into Birmingham and, hallelujah, the man opposite Cute Boy got up to go. The boy looked at me and nodded his chin at the seat opposite him. Fabola, I thought, and made my way over.

As the train lurched to a stop, I lost my balance. Given the day I was having, the next bit seemed inevitable.

'Hi,' grinned Cute Boy as I fell straight into his lap. 'Actually, I was thinking of the seat opposite. But this is OK by me.'

I could tell he expected me to leap up all embarrassed, so I decided to outcool him. I stayed where I was for a moment like I was really comfortable and gave him one of my best seduction looks – the one with a smile and one raised eyebrow.

Then I got up.

'Yeah. Maybe later,' I said as I took the seat opposite.

'Oh. OK. Right. No prob,' he said, looking flustered. 'Er, I'm Simon. Hi.'

★ ★ ★

'It was so romantic,' I said to the girls later that day as I helped myself to a salt and vinegar Pringle round at Izzie's. 'Like in a film. I just *fell* into his lap. If anyone ever makes our story, I think I'd like that guy who plays Angel in "Buffy" to play his part.'

We were in Izzie's bedroom. The train had eventually got into London at six thirty. After Mum had picked me up and I'd dropped off my stuff, I begged her to let me go out. This was urgento. Not only had I not seen the girls for three whole days, but I had *so* much to tell them.

'Your story! But you've only just met him,' said Lucy, taking a swig of Coke.

'And knowing you,' said Izzie, 'it was, like, fall accidentally on purpose.'

'It was not,' I said. 'The train lurched.'

Izzie pulled one of her 'yeah right' faces but Lucy looked all ears, she's such a romantic herself.

'So tell us all about it,' she said, settling on to the purple beanbag on Izzie's floor.

'Well, the rest of the journey whizzed by. We talked non-stop. Before we knew it, we were pulling into Euston . . .'

'What's his name?' asked Lucy.

'Simon Peddington Lee. He lives in Holland Park and he's eighteen.'

'What does he look like?' asked Izzie.

'Tall, dark and handsome. Lovely brown eyes.'

'What was he doing on the train?'

'He'd been up to have a look at St Andrews University, to see if he'd like to go there after A-levels. I've decided I might go there as well after school. It really is *the* place now.'

'That's where Prince William went isn't it? asked Lucy.

'Yep. So it's *très* posh.'

'What school does Simon go to now?' asked Lucy.

'Some private school. I forget the name. In Hampshire somewhere. He's a boarder.'

'So he's a posh boy?' said Izzie, then put on a silly snobby voice. 'Peddington Lee.'

'He's not snobby or stuck-up or anything,' I said, ignoring her. 'I told him I went to a public school as well.'

'But, Nesta,' said Lucy, 'that's a lie.'

'No, it isn't,' I said, laughing. 'Our school *is* open to the public. And I think I may change my name – you know, make it double-barrelled as well. It could be Nesta Costello-Williams by using my dad's then my mum's name. Or do you think it should be Nesta Williams-Costello?'

'Oh, don't even go there,' said Izzie. 'Just be yourself. Nesta Williams sounds just fine.'

'Nesta Top Toff Totty,' giggled Lucy.

'I thought you'd be pleased for me,' I said, feeling hurt. 'I've met someone I really like.'

'I *am* pleased,' said Lucy. 'But are you sure you want to get involved with a boy who might be going away soon?'

'Not until autumn. It's only April. Then if we still like each other I can join him up in Scotland when I finish school.'

'I thought you wanted to be an actress,' said Izzie. 'I bet they don't do drama at St Andrews.'

I hadn't thought of that. 'They might. And anyway, I think it's best to keep all your options open at our age.'

Izzie burst out laughing. 'You sound like my mum, Nesta. Did he ask to see you again?'

'Yeah. We're going riding.'

'Riding! As in horses?'

'Yeah.'

'Doh. Have you ever actually been on a horse?'

'No, but I'm sure I'll soon get the hang of it.'

Lucy and Izzie exchanged worried looks.

'You did tell him you've never ridden, didn't you?' said Lucy.

'Course not. It can't be that difficult.'

'Uhh Nesta . . .' Lucy started.

'No,' interrupted Izzie. 'She's going to have to find out for herself . . .'

Nesta's Diary

Guess what? *J'ai un* boyfriend *nouveau. Il s'appelle* Simon Peddington Lee and he's lush. He's already sent me a text message. :->> Which means 'a huge smile'. And BCNU.

I sent him back one ☺)))) Then CUL8R.

I wish I could tell the future as I think he may be The One. I haven't fancied anyone for ages. And I've never been in love. Not properly. He seems more grown up than all the rejects I've been out with in the last year and has nice legs, really long, and a *très* snoggable mouth.

Rejects since I came to *Londres*:

Robin: (1 week going out last Sept) Sweet but boring. Stares off into space in what he hopes is a cool way but I think makes him look like a right plonker.

Michael: (2 dates in October) A user and a bad snogger who likes to bite.

Nick:	(1 date in December) Disgusting. Uses too much hair gel. Has strange habit of trying to lick girls' ears out. Not pleasant.
Steve:	(Jan) Quite liked him but was juvenile and smaller than me.
Alan:	(3 weeks in Feb) Half and half. He said he wants to be a doctor and tried to put his hands down my jumper to examine any problems. Pathetic.

My brother Tony has another new girlfriend and apparently he dislocated his jaw after a snogging session. How did he manage that? I don't know whether to tell Lucy or not. Must check out state of play with them now as they were an item last year. Girls always fancy Tone but he was v. hung up on Lucy.

Izzie's having a bit of a SOHF (sense of humour failure). I don't know why as she is going out with Ben the lead singer from King Noz and is happier than ever.

Am v. v. tired. ZZZZzzzz

Chapter 2

Hard Times

Mum's been kind of quiet since I got back from Manchester. She usually sings in the morning. Badly, I have to say, but I don't tell her that. But today, she's sitting in the kitchen, reading the morning paper and not looking her usual self at all.

I pulled up a stool next to her at the breakfast bar. 'Are you missing Dad?'

'Sure,' she said. 'Course I miss him but I'm used to him working away. Why do you ask?'

I gave her my Inspector Morse 'you don't fool me' look. 'You seem a bit low. Was it because I raced off to see Lucy and Iz last night and didn't stay to catch up with you?'

Mum laughed. 'No, honey. I'm kind of used to that as well.'

'OK, then. Sure you're OK?'

'Sure,' she smiled.

'OK. Then can I have horse-riding lessons?'

'Horse-riding? Whatever for? You've never shown any interest in horses before.'

At that moment, my brother Tony trudged in. His hair was sticking up all over the place and he was still wearing his dressing-gown and yawning sleepily. 'Yeah. What do you want horse-riding lessons for? Who do you want to impress now?'

'Unlike some people present,' I said, 'I don't have to impress.'

'Some boy I expect,' continued Tony.

'Actually, I did meet a boy on the train back yesterday . . .'

'I knew it,' said Tony as he stuck his head in the fridge.

'Well, he's invited me to go riding,' I said, trying to resist the urge to push the rest of Tony into the fridge and close the door behind him.

'Where?' said Mum.

'Somewhere down near Hyde Park. Kensington, I think. He gave me the address. I've got it upstairs.'

'When?' said Tony, coming back out of the fridge with orange juice and croissants.

'Tomorrow.'

Tony plastered his croissant with raspberry jam, then sat at the bar. 'And you were like, going to learn how to ride in one afternoon? Get real.'

I stuck my tongue out at him. 'Thought you'd dislocated your jaw from snogging too much. How are you even going to chew?'

'Same way you're going to horse-ride,' he said, grimacing as he took a bite. 'With difficulty. Anyway, it's not dislocated. Just a bit sore.'

'Serves you right. I can go, can't I, Mum?' I said. 'Horse-riding?'

'Actually,' said Mum, 'I've been wanting to talk to both of you about something. I was going to wait until your dad was back, but this is as good a time as any.'

Oh *NO*, I thought. Mum and Dad are splitting up. Please *no*. I remember Izzie telling Lucy and I about when her parents separated. It started exactly the same way. She noticed her mum was unhappy. Her dad hadn't been around for days. Then the conversation, 'I've been wanting to talk to you about something.'

'No. *NO!*' I cried. 'Have you tried Relate? Marriage counselling? You *mustn't* just give up. You have to work at relationships.'

Mum and Tony stared at me as though I was mad.

'What are you on about, Nesta?' said Mum.

'Divorce. Please, *please*, for me and Tony, give it another try.'

Mum creased up laughing. 'I'm not going to get divorced, Nesta. I'm very happy with your father.'

'So what is it, then?'

Mum's expression grew serious again. 'Work. My contract is up for renewal at the beginning of next month and there's been talk of bringing in new blood at the station.'

Tony thumped the breakfast bar angrily. 'New as in younger?'

Mum nodded.

'Pathetic,' said Tony. 'How can they? You're the face of the evening news. They *can't* replace you.'

Mum put her hand over Tony's. 'Oh yes they can, honey. It happens all the time. Producers want better ratings – they're always looking for ways to bring in more viewers.'

'Well, I don't think it helps to get rid of some of their best people. You read the news really well,' said Tony.

Mum smiled at him. 'Thanks, kid. You wanna be my agent?'

'It wouldn't be the same if you didn't do the news,' I said. 'It's like, the next best thing to you being at home when I get back from school. I always switch on the telly when I'm having my tea and there you are in the corner to say hello to.'

'When will you know?' asked Tony.

'In the next few weeks. But this is what I wanted to talk to you about. It means tightening the purse strings.

We're going to have to economise.'

'We'll be all right,' I said. 'Dad earns loads of money. And he's still working.'

'That's why I was going to wait until he was here,' said Mum. 'You're right, he does earn good money *when* he's working. But, don't forget, he's a *freelance* director. That means if he's working, he gets paid. If he's not, he doesn't. And we did rather overextend ourselves buying this flat.'

'But why is it different now?' I asked.

'Because *my* job is insecure, that's what I'm trying to tell you. He finishes his film in Manchester in the next few weeks and, so far, he hasn't got anything else lined up. See, it didn't matter in the past as my regular income helped us ride those times. But now . . .'

'OhmyGod,' I groaned. 'We're *poor*. Oh, God.'

My mind was swimming with images. *Poor? No* pocket money. *No* trips out to the movies. *No* more McDonald's. I'd be the one out in the rain with my nose pressed up against the window watching rich people in nice clothes eat nourishing meals in the warm. And I'd be outside in rags, cold . . . hungry . . .

Mum laughed again. 'We're not poor yet, Nesta. We still have a roof over our heads. And food to eat. All I'm saying is that until things are more certain, there won't be any money for extras.'

'So no horse-riding lessons?'

'Exactly. No horse-riding lessons,' said Mum.

'But I can go and meet Simon?'

'As long as you're home for supper. Yes, you can go and meet this Simon.'

'But won't you need money to go and meet Simon?' said Tony, trying to stir it as usual.

'No I won't, smartypants,' I replied. 'He's known the lady that owns the stables all his life. He told me all about her on the train. He teaches some of the young kids that go there at the weekend. In exchange, she lets him and his friends ride whenever they like. For free. So there.'

'So why did you want horse-riding lessons if he could teach you?' asked Tony, doing one of his all-knowing smug faces. 'Oh I see, you wanted to show off, like, yeah, I'm Nesta Williams and I've been riding all my life . . .'

'I did not.'

'Did.'

'Didn't.'

'Did.'

'When will you two grow up?' asked Mum, putting her hands over her ears.

Chapter 3

Me and
Robert Redford

I'd arranged to meet Simon at High Street Kensington tube as he said it was near the stables. I was really looking forward to it – a whole afternoon on my own with him. It would be a chance to get to know him better. And it wouldn't cost anything.

I got to Kensington station, ran up the stairs, past *Prêt à Manger* and the Sock Shop in the tube entrance, then out to the High Street – and there my heart sank. Simon was waiting with two tall, slim, blonde girls. They were about the same age as me, maybe a year older, and both were slouching against the rails outside the station doing that pouty 'I'm so bored' *Vogue* model look. They looked like experienced riders with their hair tied back, jodhpurs and riding boots. Both of them looked at me as if I was an alien.

I was wearing my Levis, Nike trainers and my psycho babe top. It's really cool. On the front it has a picture of a trendy girl with psychedelic eyes that swirl about. On the back, is written 'All stressed out and no one to choke'.

'This is my sister, Tanya,' said Simon. 'And this is her friend, Cressida.'

Tanya smiled, but Cressida did a sort of posh grimace and looked disdainfully at my T-shirt.

'So you're Nesta?' she drawled.

'The one and only,' I grinned. 'Hi.'

Tanya looked nice, with an open friendly face like Simon's. Cressida, on the other hand, looked as though she had a bad smell under her nose. Shame, because she would have been quite pretty otherwise.

As we set off in the direction of the park, I felt in a really good mood. It was a lovely spring day, and the daffs and tulips were out in the park. And I was with Simon.

Cressida and Tanya trailed along beside us talking into their mobile phones and I could see Cressida watching my every move. When Simon reached out and took my hand, she looked positively horrified.

'You *did* say you'd ridden before, didn't you?' asked Simon.

'Yeah, I did, but to be honest, no, I haven't. I thought I could wing it. It can't be that hard, surely? You just get on the horse. Check your rear mirror and pull out into oncoming traffic.'

Simon cracked up. 'No prob. I'll show you. And actually, you're not that far from the truth. We do have to take the horses a short distance on the road from the stables to the park.'

'On the road!' I wasn't sure I liked the sound of that. 'But what about traffic?'

'Don't worry, the horses are used to the cars and most motorists know to go slow round here. And we'll find you a nice horse. One who won't give you a hard time.'

'Oh, OK. Cool,' I said, but I was beginning to feel a bit nervous.

'You mean you've *never* been on a horse *ever*?' sneered Cressida, catching us up.

I was about to say, 'You. Off my planet,' but I bit my tongue and shook my head in response to her question. I've met her type before and have little time for them, but she was a friend of Simon's and I didn't want to embarrass him.

The stables were tucked away from the main road down a cobbled mews. On the corner was a small stable block with horses looking out over the individual doors.

'Amazing to find this here,' I said. 'I never even knew you could ride in London. I thought you had to go to Devon or Cornwall.'

'I know. Good, isn't it?' said Tanya. 'We've been coming

here since we were little but loads of people don't know it's here.'

'There's been riding in Hyde Park for three hundred years so it's not new,' said Simon.

'Wow. Three hundred years,' I said. 'Impressive.'

Cressida did her snooty look for the nth time that day. 'I prefer to ride in Richmond,' she said. 'My cousin has stables there and that's where all the real riders go. One's so aware that one's in town here whereas in Richmond it's more countrified.'

I felt like saying, Why don't you bog off there, then? (Or rather, in her language, why doesn't one bog orf there, then? Like yah spiffy bonce.) But again I bit my tongue.

A lady came out of what looked like an office and waved hello.

'The lady with the blonde hair, that's the one I told you about, Mrs Creighton,' said Simon, waving back. 'She'll sort you out a good horse. I'll just go and have a word. Come on, Tanya, you can help me saddle up.'

They strode off, leaving me with Sour Puss.

'Aren't you going to change?' she asked.

'No. People tend to like me the way I am,' I grinned.

'But you're not riding like *that*, are you?'

'Sure,' I said. 'Why not?'

'Well, it's not standard,' said Cressida.

I glared at her. 'And your point is?'

We stood there for a while in uncomfortable silence. I wished Lucy and Izzie were there, then we'd all have been beginners together and had a laugh.

Tanya came forward and gave me a hard riding hat. 'Put this on, Nesta. You'll have to wear a hat in case you fall. It'll protect your head.'

I put on the hat and turned to see Simon leading a chestnut brown horse with a white star on his forehead towards us.

'Here we go,' he grinned. 'Mrs Creighton says this is the boy for you.'

Cressida snorted with laughter. 'Heddie! You're putting Nesta on Heddie! But he's *ancient*!'

'It's her first time,' said Simon, patting Heddie on the neck. 'We don't want to put her on a horse that will take off with her.'

Cressida looked as if that's *exactly* what she wanted.

'Come on, Nesta, let's get you up. Then we'll take it real slow,' said Simon.

As I took a step towards the horse, my 'oh, I can wing it' philosophy changed to 'if you can't beat 'em, make a run for it'. I felt *really* nervous. Heddie looked enormous. I mean, I'm tall for my age but my head only came up above Heddie's legs. How was I ever going to get up on him? I made myself breathe deeply like we do in drama to calm our nerves and took another step towards him.

He blew dust and shuffled back.

Out of the corner of my eye, I could see Cressida enjoying every minute of my discomfort. I'll show you, I thought. I may not have ridden a horse before, but I *have* read Izzie's copy of *Feel the Fear and Do It Anyway* – well, the first three pages. I decided that's exactly what I'd do. I stood tall, felt the fear and strode towards the horse with every ounce of confidence I could muster.

'OK,' said Simon, smiling at me reassuringly. 'Take it real slow. Put your foot in the stirrup. Good. Lift yourself up over Heddie, then, when you're ready, lift your other leg over.'

I did as he told me, but didn't feel I could haul myself over. I got my left foot in the stirrup, but couldn't get a grip to pull the rest of me up so I was sort of hopping around on one leg like a total prat. Luckily Simon came to the rescue and gave me a push up. And guess what? Suddenly I was on the horse. High off the ground. Scary. But, once I got my balance, brilliant.

Tanya came out of the stables with two horses, a grey one and a black one, and Cressida disappeared, presumably to get hers.

Simon took the reins of the grey horse. 'Stay where you are, Nesta. I'll get on Prince then we'll go.'

No problem, I thought as Simon mounted his horse gracefully. I ain't going nowhere.

Whooaghhhh.

Apparently I was.

Heddie had taken it into his head to have a drink of water and wandered over to a trough outside the stable in the mews.

Whoooooah.

He bent his head down to drink and I started to slide forward. I thought I was going to go over his shoulders and held on for dear life. Of course Cressida came out at that moment, looking fab on a stunning white horse. She looked at me with disapproval then nodded to Tanya and the two of them trotted off and disappeared down the mews to the road leading into the park.

'Wait for us,' called Simon, trotting over to me. 'You're doing really well, Nesta. Just pull on the rein gently and he'll come up.'

I did what he said but Heddie took no notice. I pulled again. Still no reaction. Simon took the reins from me and up Heddie came.

'Sometimes they can tell if someone's a bit nervous,' he said.

'Me? Nervous? Nah,' I said. 'Born to ride.'

Inside I was shaking.

Mrs Creighton came over a moment later and looked at me kindly. 'I'll lead you until you get into the park,' she asked. 'It can be a bit nerve-racking going alongside traffic your first time.'

Thank God. I hadn't been sure how long I could have kept up the bravado act.

It felt weird being high above the cars as we walked towards the park but I felt safe with Mrs Creighton leading Heddie and Simon just in front. Once we got through the park gates, she let go.

'We never let a beginner out without an instructor,' she said. 'And Simon's taught a lot of my pupils so you're in safe hands.'

'Don't even think of getting up any speed today,' he said after she'd gone. 'Just try to get comfortable with the feel of the horse.'

'No prob,' I said. 'I think Heddie's OK with me now.'

'If you're sure you're OK for a second,' said Simon, 'I'm just going to ride ahead, only for a minute or two, to check on Tanya. I promised Mum I'd keep an eye on her and she does tend to get carried away, especially when she's with Cressida. Cress does a lot of competition riding and likes to show off a bit.'

'Fine,' I said. 'You go ahead.'

'Don't go anywhere,' he insisted.

As he cantered off and disappeared round a corner, I imagined myself playing the part of a country heroine in a period drama. I could be Tess of the d'Urbevilles. Or Jane Eyre. Or maybe in a modern drama. I could be in *The Horse Whisperer* with Robert Redford. I could be the daughter who learns to ride again after her horrible accident.

Suddenly Heddie swung to the left, bent over and started chewing grass by the side of the track. Once again, I almost slid off his shoulders, this time into a rhododendron bush. I gripped my knees and pulled hard on the reins. 'Come on, Heddie. This isn't in the script. Come on, there's a good boy. Up you come.'

Heddie took no notice. I pulled again. He pulled against me.

I knew from watching *The Horse Whisperer* that it's best not to get aggressive. Horses respond to kindness. Clearly I'd have to do some horse-whispering.

I bent forward and stroked Heddie's neck. 'Come on, boy. Lovely boy. Handsome boy,' I whispered. 'Up you come.'

No response. Maybe he didn't speak English.

'Hoopla,' I whispered. 'Aley oop. Venez upwardos. Muchos gratios stoppee eatee grassee.'

I heard someone laughing behind me. It was Simon.

'What on earth are you doing?'

'Durrh. Horse-whispering. What else?'

He burst out laughing. 'Honestly, Nesta, you crease me up. Is he giving you a hard time?'

'Sort of. He thinks it's lunch-time.'

Once again, Simon pulled the reins and up Heddie came.

'Hold on to the reins and we'll try a bit of trotting,' said Simon. 'Sit straight. Give a gentle dig with your heels and then try to rise and fall in time with the horse as he goes along.'

Off we went. After a few bumps, I found the rhythm. Up and down I went. I was doing OK.

As we turned a corner, I saw a tree about ten metres ahead and slightly to the left of us with its branches sticking out into the path. Simon rode to the right to avoid it and I tried to steer Heddie to do the same. But no, he wasn't having any of it. He was heading straight for the branch, or rather, *he* was heading straight under the branch. I tried to duck but it was too low. It was going to hit me straight in the tummy.

Next thing I knew, I was in midair, hanging on to the branch as Heddie trotted off without me.

'*Simon!*' I cried.

Simon turned and gasped.

As I hung there, I suddenly got a fit of giggles. 'I think I've really got the hang of it now,' I said.

Simon got off his horse and came towards me. 'Here, let me help you down.' Then he got the giggles as well. 'Oh, I wish I had a camera,' he said. 'I could put a photo of you dangling there in my album with the caption: *Nesta goes horse-riding.*'

'Or *Nesta branches out from horse-riding*,' I laughed as he helped me to the ground and took a leaf out of my hair.

'Or *Nesta takes a leaf out of her book when it comes to horse-riding*,' I said.

We were bent over laughing as Cressida trotted up to join us.

'We were wondering where you'd got to,' she said, looking very disgruntled that we were having a good time. 'What are you doing?'

'Oh, just hanging out,' I said and that started us laughing again.

Simon quickly told Cressida what had happened and she laughed as well. But at me, not *with* me.

I felt hurt. I mean, she'd obviously been riding for years. I reckoned she could have been a bit kinder seeing as I was a beginner.

Then the penny dropped. Oh *I* get it, I thought. There's some history between them. Either she fancies Simon or they've been out together in the past. I wonder what happened?

Nesta's Diary

Went horse-riding today. Fabola. Simon was a brill rider and looked incredibly sexy in his riding boots. After we'd finished we went and had a cappuccino at the Dome by High Street Kensington. By now his sister and her Pedigree Chum Cressida (I think I'll call her Watercress) had got the message and cleared orf. The way they talk is hysterical. Simon and Tanya aren't too bad but Cressida talks like she's got a ping-pong ball stuck in her gobbette.

Me and Simon had our first snog at the tube. *Très bien*. Gentle. He's a good kisser, eight out of ten. Not bad for a start. We didn't want to get too carried away because there was a crowd of tourists staring at us and one even took a photograph. Cheek. Of course that will be worth money in a few years' time when I'm famous.

Chapter 4

Pedigree Chums

'But Mum . . .'

'No buts, Nesta. I thought I'd made it clear to you . . .'

'Yeah, but you don't understand. It's really important to have the right gear. I have to look the part. This is more important than *anything* I've ever done in my life before.'

Mum laughed and said, 'N. O. No.'

'*Please*, Mum. Just this and then I promise I'll never ask for anything else. Ever. *And* I'll clear up.' I rolled up my sleeves, cleared some dishes and started loading the dishwasher.

Mum sighed and cleared away the remaining dishes from the table. 'No, Nesta. I know it's hard but until things are more settled, the answer's no. You'll be fine riding in a pair of chinos and a T-shirt.'

'It's not fair. Why do we have to run out of money just at the exact time I make friends with people who have loads of it?'

'Welcome to the world, kid,' said Mum. 'Sometimes life isn't fair.'

'Mum doesn't even try to understand,' I said to Lucy and Izzie later when we met at Lucy's house. 'She could easily sell something. The car or something.'

Lucy gasped. 'Nesta!'

'What? *What?*' I said. 'I was only joking. Not the car. But I'm sure there's something we could sell so I can get kitted out. You *have* to have the right gear to be taken seriously.'

'Says who?' said Izzie's voice from behind the sofa. 'I think all this "right gear or you're not a serious rider" stuff is pants. Who *says* you have to wear this or you're a reject? People like Cressida, that's who. And she sounds like a right snotty cow.'

'What are you doing, Iz?' I asked, looking over the sofa.

In the gap between the sofa and the wall, Izzie was standing on her head. 'Headstand.'

'Yeah. I can see that.'

'Yoga,' said Iz. 'Supposed to do ten minutes a day to let the blood flow to my brain. It's to aid relaxation.'

Looks like it does exactly the opposite, I thought as I settled on the sofa to do my nails like a sensible person.

Yoga is Izzie's new thing. Personally I think it's a bit anti-social. Like, you'll be in the middle of a conversation and suddenly she'll start wrapping her leg round the back of her neck. Or she'll lie on the floor and roll up on to her shoulders and you find yourself talking to her butt.

'I think I've seen a pair of jodhpurs in the spare room,' came The Voice From Behind The Sofa. 'One of the Ugly Sisters' cast-offs. Want me to check when I get home?'

The Ugly Sisters are Izzie's stepsisters Claudia and Amelia. They're in their twenties so don't live at Izzie's any more but both of them seem to have left clothes there for when they visit.

'Does Robbie Williams have a tattoo? Course I do,' I said. 'Thanks. It really is awful being poor, you know.'

For some reason this made Izzie laugh and she lost her balance and came up from behind the sofa. 'You don't half talk tosh sometimes, Nesta. Poor is having no food. No home. No clothes.'

'Exactly,' I replied. 'No clothes.'

Izzie tossed her hair impatiently. 'Not designer clothes, dummy.'

'Easy to say, but you know what it's like at school. If you don't have the right trainers you get slagged off.'

'So what?' said Izzie. 'The people who slag you off for something so stupid as what brand of trainers you have or haven't, are total morons.'

'And you don't let people like that get to you, do you?' asked Lucy.

I shrugged. Sometimes I acted braver than I felt. 'How do you manage, Lucy?'

'Don't look at me,' she said, looking taken aback. 'We may not be rich, but we're not poor.'

'Nesta! Sometimes you should think before you open that big mouth of yours,' said Izzie.

Iz and Lucy have known each other since junior school, longer than I've known them both as I only joined their school last September. Izzie always confronts anyone she thinks might hurt Lucy. Even me. Even me when I'm *completely* innocent.

'But . . .' I started.

'It's OK,' said Lucy. 'I'm not offended.'

'I wasn't being insulting, Izzie. I was asking advice. What's wrong with that? We all know that Lucy gets less pocket money than us. And she hasn't as much money for clothes.'

'Yeah, but Lucy might not want it broadcasted to the whole world.'

'Excuse *me*, but I am actually *here*,' said Lucy, 'like, in person. And it's cool. I don't mind you two knowing that my parents aren't as well off as yours or, sorry Nesta, yours *were*. And you know how I manage. I make my own clothes. And sometimes I babysit. Why not try that?'

'Oh, get real,' I said. 'I need a lot more money than I could earn babysitting.'

This time Lucy did look offended and Izzie gave me one of her 'mess with my mate and you're dead' looks.

'What? *What?*' I asked.

'So you're clearly not *that* desperate, then,' said Izzie. 'Really poor people take what work they can. And for your information, you can earn quite a lot babysitting.'

Eek. The atmosphere was starting to feel really uncomfortable. There's only one way out of this, I thought. When the going gets tough, the tough resort to being silly.

'Oh, come orf it,' I said, doing my best impression of the Queen. 'One is only trying to say that one *must* have other options.'

Thank God, both of them laughed.

'Look, I know it's hard,' said Lucy, 'when you really want something badly and you can't have it. You're not the first to discover horse-riding, you know. A couple of years ago, I wanted lessons, but they cost thirty quid a time. No way Mum and Dad could pay for that.'

'So what did you do?'

'I had to forget about it.'

'When I'm rich and famous,' I said, '*I'll* pay for you to have lessons.'

'At least Simon can help you with that side of things,' said Izzie, settling on the floor and criss-crossing her legs into the lotus position. 'You don't have to worry about lessons.'

'I know, he was fab. I was more nervous than I let on and to tell the truth, I felt like crying when I couldn't get on the horse and Watercress was laughing at me hopping about with one foot stuck in the stirrup. I didn't let her see I was upset though.'

'Why are you bothered about impressing a creep like her? Sounds like Simon couldn't care less whether you turned up barefoot or in Gucci gumboots – and he's the one that matters.'

'I just want to show her that she can't intimidate me. That I'm as good as she is.'

'Why?' said Iz. 'You don't even like her.'

'Yeah,' said Lucy. 'Remember that quote on one of Mum's Angel Cards last year. "No one can make you feel inferior without your permission." Saying you want to prove that you're as good as Cressida means that you think she's better than you. It's like you've given her permission to make you feel inferior.'

I was getting confused. I didn't want to talk about it any more. I thought they'd understand how I felt, but they didn't. And to tell the truth, neither did I.

'Oh, let's watch the DVD,' I said, hoping to change the subject. 'You're both way too deep for me.'

We spent the next half hour watching Lucy's DVD about a man called Monty Roberts. He's the guy that the character

Robert Redford played in *The Horse Whisperer* is based on, only Monty does it for real. Lucy got it as a Christmas present when she was going through her horse-mad phase.

'So the general idea is not look the horse in the eyes as that's seen as a challenge,' I said after watching the film.

'Yeah. And to let him know that you're not a threat,' said Lucy.

'Be friendly but confident,' said Izzie as she tried to come out of her lotus position. Sadly, her legs had gone numb from sitting in such a strange position for so long and she couldn't stand up. She sank back on to the carpet with her legs and arms in the air.

'And what position is that in yoga?' I asked. 'The dead dog?'

'If you're afraid, horses pick up on it,' continued Lucy as Izzie lay on the floor moaning, 'and it makes them afraid. So the trick is to be cool.'

'Cool,' I said. 'Confident. That's me.'

'Cool,' cried Izzie. 'Oh *God*. Aghhh. Now I've got pins and needles. Help. *I'm in agony!*'

So much for yoga for relaxation, I thought.

'Shall we get another DVD?' asked Lucy.

'Can't,' I said. 'Got a date.'

'Where are you going?' asked Izzie.

'Movie. I said I'd meet Simon at the cinema on the King's Road at six thirty.'

Izzie looked at her watch. 'Six *thirty*! Nesta, it's five fifteen.'

'Oh pants! I lost track of time watching that film. Now I won't have time to go home and get changed!'

'You'd better get going now,' said Lucy, helping Iz up on to the sofa, 'or you'll never make it. It'll take you at least an hour to get there.'

Outside it was raining. I looked at Izzie and Lucy curled up all cosily on the sofa and felt really tempted to call off my date. A night here with the girls suddenly looked like a better option. Plus Lucy's brothers would be back later and they're a real laugh.

I quickly dialled Simon's mobile number. 'Pants. It's on answer service.'

'You'd better go,' said Lucy. 'You don't want to stand him up.'

'Come with me,' I asked. 'In case the Pedigree Chums are there as well.'

'Pedigree Chums?' asked Lucy.

'Tanya and her horrid mate.'

Izzie looked out of the window at the rain and pulled a face.

'We'll walk you to the tube,' said Lucy. 'It's on the way to the pizza shop. Come on, Iz. Get the brollies. Do you want to borrow a jacket, Nesta? You'll freeze in only a T-shirt.'

She held out her silver jacket for me, but it was way too small.

'Or you could borrow one of Steve or Lal's?' she said, offering me a choice of two hideously naff anoraks.

'As if,' I said. 'I'm not turning up looking like a total plonker.'

Izzie put on Lal's jacket and Lucy put on Steve's and we set off for the tube. After only five minutes I was soaked.

'You have to borrow a jacket,' said Lucy. 'You'll freeze. Do you want the maroon or the orange?'

I had no choice. 'Maroon,' I said miserably. '*Maroon!* My life as a style queen is over.'

I hope Simon realises the sacrifices I'm making for him, I thought as I emerged at Sloane Street tube about an hour later. Trust me to go and fall for someone who lives on the other side of the planet.

I asked the man outside the tube selling the *Evening Standard* where the cinema was and he pointed to the left of the square.

'Down the King's Road, duck,' he said. 'Best get a bus in this rain.'

As I ran in the direction of the bus stop, I tried to think of an appropriate film that I could imagine I was starring in. I find that pretending to be someone else helps me to get through difficult situations sometimes, but I couldn't think of any film where the heroine trawls over London in the rain in the anorak from hell.

The bus came after a few minutes and as I got on, I asked the driver to give me a shout when we got to the cinema. I took a seat and soon we were whizzing past shops and cafés down the King's Road.

Living in London is still new to me. We came to live here last summer when Mum got a job reading the news on Cable. Before that we lived in Bristol, which was OK, but nothing like this. I keep discovering more and more of it – different areas, and each one has its own atmosphere. It's brillopad.

'Cinema!' shouted the bus driver.

As I got off the bus I couldn't see Simon or the Pedigree Chums. I quickly took off the naff jacket as I didn't want them to see me in it.

A few more minutes went by. I hope I haven't missed them, I thought. I checked my watch. I was ten minutes late. Surely they'd have waited? We'd only have missed the commercials.

Another five minutes passed. Then another five. I was freezing. So much for the coming spring; it had turned back into winter. Well, this afternoon's been a total waste of make-up, I thought, as I put Lal's jacket back on and started to walk back to the bus stop.

'*Nesta!*' Simon's voice called.

I looked across the road and there he was, waving frantically. He ran across to join me.

'So sorry we're late,' he panted. 'Traffic. Couldn't park anywhere.'

'Been waiting long?' said Cressida, coming up behind him and looking like she couldn't care less how long I'd been waiting.

'No, I just got here,' I said, then turned to Simon. 'Hey, this place is great. I haven't been down here before.'

I could see Cressida sneering again. One of these days, I thought, I really must ask her what the bad smell is that seems to be perpetually under her nose.

'It *used* to be great,' she said, 'but Notting Hill is the place to shop now.' She looked disdainfully at Lal's jacket. 'But then I don't expect you've been there either, have you?'

She did look amazing, I have to say. She had a cropped white leather jacket on and the most amazing pair of black patent ankle boots – really high with peep toes. My soggy trainers looked so unglamorous beside them.

'I only moved to London last summer,' I said. 'We were in Los Angeles before, so it's all very new to me.' She doesn't need to know it was only for a week's holiday, I thought.

For a second Cressida looked impressed. 'How come you lived there?'

'My dad's a film director,' I said.

'Has he made anything we'd know?' asked Tanya, who'd been off getting the tickets. She looked fab as well in a leather mini and DKNY T-shirt. I was starting to feel way underdressed.

'Oh, loads. Course, it helps having Spielberg as an uncle.'

Now Cressida did look impressed. And it wasn't a lie. I just didn't mention I meant Leister Spielberg not Steven. He's married to my aunt and runs a dry cleaner's over there.

'How did you get here?' asked Simon.

'Tube then bus. Took ages.'

'You came by *bus*?' sneered Cressida.

Oh, here we go, I thought. 'Well, how else from North London?'

'Taxi, of course.'

I wasn't in the mood. 'Dahling,' I said in my best posh voice, 'anyone who's *anyone* knows that buses *are* the new taxi. Taxis are so *nineties*. Buses are the thing, the new cool way to travel.'

Simon hooted with laughter and joined in. 'Absolutely, dahling. In fact, the number eighty-eight is my favourite.'

Even Tanya laughed, but old Watercress scowled and pulled Tanya away to queue for popcorn.

'That's one of the things I really like about you,' said Simon.

'What?' I asked.

'Your attitude. You're so confident. It's brilliant.'

Just as well he couldn't see what was going on in my head. It was far from confident. For some reason Cressida really bugged me. It was weird. What Lucy said was true; I gave Cressida permission to make me feel inferior. That confident attitude Simon saw? It was acting.

Nesta's Diary

Simon gave me a lift home after he'd dropped the Pedigree Chums off. He lives in Holland Park in a white house behind some black railings. It looked v. posh. He asked if I wanted to go in but I wasn't up for meeting his mum or dad when I was dressed in my jeans and wearing Lal's jacket.

Simon says they also have another house in Wiltshire where they keep horses. I told him we used to keep hamsters up until a few years ago. He completely cracked up laughing. I don't think he realised I was serious about the hamsters.

He's got a fab car. A black Volkswagon. He put the Manic Street Preachers on really loud and when we got to my street we sat and snogged for ages until Tony came past and knocked on the window, giving both of us the shock of our lives.

I have decided to shorten Cressida's nickname from Watercress to WC. Tanya is much nicer than WC, much more friendly. I asked her where they got their clothes from and she said all over really, sometimes Selfridges, sometimes Gucci in Bond Street, sometimes DKNY but mostly from the designer shops around Portobello Road.

I'm going to Notting Hill tomorrow with Iz and Lucy. I'm looking forward to it as it's another bit of London I've never been to and I know there's a famous song about Portobello Road. Saturrrdayee morning. That's it.

I wish I could afford to buy some new gear.

Chapter 5

Portobello Princesses

The next day, I drew thirty pounds out of my savings and set off for Notting Hill with the girls. We got off at Ladbroke Grove tube and headed up behind the market. Tanya had told me that's where the good boutiques were.

'Doesn't look as posh as Knightsbridge, does it?' said Lucy, staring at the white terraced houses on the way.

'No,' said Izzie, 'but it is. Loads of celebrities live here now.'

'My mum says that houses can go for as much as four million,' said Izzie.

'You'd have to win the Lottery to live here, then,' said Lucy.

After roads of terraced houses, we passed some amazing antique shops, full of enormous gold frames and mirrors big enough to fill a whole wall.

'Bit different from Homebase,' said Izzie, gazing in at

one window crammed with chandeliers made from moulded glass flames and wrought iron.

'And – *wow* – look at these shoes,' I said as we came across a shop called Emma Hope on the corner of one street. 'They're so pretty, like made for fairytale princesses.'

'Portobello Princesses,' said Izzie, looking at a shop further down. 'You need to be royalty to afford the prices.'

'Portobello Princesses,' I laughed. 'I like that. That describes Cressida and Tanya *exactly*.'

We spent the first ten minutes window shopping, looking in a shop called Joseph and another called Rikki, then at the end of the row, a window display caught my eye. 'Now *this* looks interesting.'

'No,' said Lucy. 'I don't want to go in.'

'Why not?'

'Doesn't look friendly. And there's no one else in there.'

'Oh, don't be silly,' I said and dragged her up the steps to the shop. I pushed the door but it was closed. Inside a stick-thin assistant looked up and indicated we should ring the bell.

I rang the bell and the door bleeped open.

'I'm going to wander down towards the market,' said Lucy, pulling away. 'I'll meet you later.'

'Lucy,' I whispered to her as I shoved her into the shop,

'what was it you were saying to me about people only being able to make you feel inferior if you give them permission? You belong here as much as the next person. In fact, you'll probably run a place like this when you're up and running as a designer.'

'I doubt it,' said Lucy, looking around. '*I'm* going to make my customers feel welcome.'

Inside, it was all concrete and chrome with lilac tube lighting, sort of minimal so it did look a bit cold. And the assistant was eyeing us suspiciously. But the clothes on the rails looked the biz boz. We had a rummage around and there were loads of things I liked. I really wanted to get something special to wear on my next date with Simon. So far, he'd only seen me in jeans and trainers. Next time, I was determined to make an impression.

'Oh, *chulo chulo*. Look at this,' I said, pulling out an amazing orange chain-mail sleeveless tank top. '*Got* to have it.'

I quickly glanced at the price. Twenty three pounds fifty. I could afford it *and* have some money left over.

I went into the changing room and tried it on. It did look fantastic. The fabric was stunning: little silky cubes all sewn together.

'Let's see,' said Lucy, sticking her head in the cubicle. '*Très* sexy.'

'Must have,' I said.

'Musto must have,' agreed Lucy.

I got changed into my own clothes and took the top over to the cash desk.

The assistant took it from me and looked at the label.

'Cash or card?'

'Cash,' I said, getting out my money and handing her three ten-pound notes.

She took them but seemed to be waiting for something.

'What?' I said.

'I need another two hundred and five pounds,' she said, as she showed me the label. It said two hundred and thirty-five pounds. Not twenty-three pounds fifty.

I wanted to die.

'Er, bit more than I thought,' I stuttered and quickly put the top back on the rails, before joining Izzie at the other end of the shop.

'What a rip-off,' said Izzie, picking out a skirt. 'This is *only* a bit of cotton and it's a *hundred* and eighty-five pounds.'

'Perhaps you'd like to look at our sale rail,' said the assistant, coming up behind us.

We trooped over to the sale rail where Izzie proceeded to embarrass me further.

'*Blimey*. Come and look at this, Lucy,' she exclaimed as she held up a strapless pink dress. 'You could make one better than this. This is eighty-five quid and that's in the *sale*!'

Honestly. Izzie goes on about me and my big mouth but she can be worse than me if she wants to be.

I wandered to the back of the shop to look at the shoes and boots. There was a pair there just like the ones WC had on the night before. I picked them up and gulped. Four hundred and ninety-five pounds! That's like, almost a *year's* pocket money! And that was only WC's boots. Lord knows what the rest of her outfit cost.

The assistant was watching us like we were kids on the nick and I suddenly remembered that scene in *Pretty Woman*. The film where Julia Roberts is shopping in posh dress shops and the assistants give her a hard time and she gets intimidated. Then she goes back looking fabulosa and a half, gives *them* a hard time then swans out and spends a fortune in another shop.

That's my film for today, I thought and tossed my hair back.

'Not really our style, is it?' I said loudly. 'Let's get a cab home and see if Daddy will fly us over to Paris in the helicopter.'

Izzie and Lucy gawped at me. Then Iz caught on.

'Yah. *Super* idea, dahling,' she said. 'This place is so, so . . .'

And we both wrinkled our noses and said, '*nineties*'.

With that, Izzie and I flounced out of the door, followed by Lucy who looked like she wanted to die. Poor Lucy. She isn't the coolest cube in the ice tray at the best of times and she'd gone a brighter red than usual.

We ran round the corner and bent over laughing.

'Did you *see* the assistant's face?' I said.

'Yes, I did,' said Lucy, punching me. 'Honestly, you don't half show me up sometimes.'

'We were only having a laugh,' said Iz. 'But what a rip-off, eh?'

'Yeah,' I agreed, 'but the clothes are something else, you have to admit.'

'They might make you feel good for a moment,' said Izzie as we set off towards the market, 'but they don't give lasting happiness.'

'What *are* you on about, Izzie?' I asked.

'Buddhism,' explained Lucy. 'Izzie's become a Buddhist like Ben. She told me all about it when you went off to the cinema last night.'

I laughed. 'You should do a single, you know, like Bob the Builder? You could sing Ben the Buddhist to the same tune only with windchimes and chanting as well and maybe dolphins in the background. It'd probably go straight to number one.' I started singing, 'Ben the Buddhist, Ben the Buddhist', then did my dolphin impersonation, 'dwoink, *bverk*, squeak'.

Lucy giggled and even Izzie cracked after a minute's trying to keep a straight face.

'OK, then,' I asked. 'So why would being a Buddhist mean you can't wear nice clothes?'

'It doesn't,' said Izzie. 'You can wear what you like to be a Buddhist. But it *does* teach that the root of all unhappiness is desire. And, mostly, desire is never-ending. Like, you get one thing, it makes you happy for a moment, then up comes another desire and you're dissatisfied again until *that* desire is satisfied and so on.'

'Yeah, I suppose,' I said. 'But so what?'

Izzie sighed impatiently. 'Ben says that in the West, we're all lost in desire, drowning in materialism.'

'Yeah. *Top*, isn't it?' I said as I spied another interesting boutique and went to look in the window. 'Drown *me* in it anytime.'

'Let's go and look at the market,' pleaded Lucy. 'I don't think I could face another of those stuck-up shops.'

She pulled me away and we headed off in the direction of Portobello Road. On the way, we passed a health shop and of course Izzie had to stop and look.

Health shops aren't really my thing but she'd come to my shop and fair's only fair so we trooped in the door. Once inside, we found there were three floors selling every variety of health food ever made. The place was so Izzie. She was in heaven, but try as I might, organic turnips just don't do it for me. There was fruit, vegetables, grains, nuts, a floor with books and aromatherapy oils and soaps and lotions, then another floor with fresh juices and healthy-type meals. I was bored after five minutes. I mean, who wants to look at millet when you can look at make-up?

'I wish we had a place like this near us,' said Iz, after we'd had a good look round. 'It's wonderful.'

'Yeah, right,' I said. 'Let's go.'

'See, places like this are what it's all about,' continued Izzie as she picked some organic chocolate off the shelf and took it to the pay counter. 'Feeds your soul as well as your body.'

'Seven pounds fifty,' said the girl at the till.

Izzie's jaw dropped open in shock as she counted out the coins from her purse.

'*Most* of the stuff in there is a bargain,' she said sheepishly when we got back out on the pavement.

I shook my head sadly. 'Wot a reep-off,' I said in my best Indian guru accent. 'That sweetie thing will only give you temporary happiness. You are lost in chocolatey desire but in an hour, oh deary me, desire will rise again. Probably for a burger. With extra onion. Or a milkshake. With big fat flakey things. Such is the nature of Western man who is drowning in illusion.'

'Then you won't be wanting any, will you, Barmy

55

Swami?' said Izzie, handing Lucy a piece of the chocolate, then running off down the road.

We spent the next couple of hours cruising Portobello Road and having the most brilliant time. The street was literally jammed with people eagerly looking at what was on sale at the many colourful stalls there. Here, there really were bargains. Pashminas, jewellery, picture frames, antiques, clothes, CDs, *everything*.

Lucy bought a fab 1940s dress from a stall selling vintage clothes. It was a soft cream voile and she said she could use the material for an idea she had. Lucy wants to be a dress designer when she leaves school. She's mega-talented. She gets old clothes and sews them together with bits of new to make really original things. Already you can see her individual style and I'm sure in years to come, people will know exactly what a Lucy Lovering creation looks like.

Izzie bought some pink flip-flops with beads and sequins from a hippie-dippie Indian stall and I bought an amazing little transparent handbag with a pink feather trim – fluffy and girlie and only four pounds ninety-nine.

'It's the way you wear 'em,' I said as I posed down the street with my new bag, doing my Marilyn Monroe wiggle.

★ ★ ★

By four o'clock we'd pretty well done the market so we decided to walk down to look at the big shops on Kensington High Street. After an hour there even I, Queen Shopaholic, was starting to feel exhausted.

'One more stop before home,' I said, leading the girls down a side street behind the tube. 'There's a shop that sells riding gear down here somewhere. Simon told me about it.'

'Well, don't get jodhpurs,' said Izzie. 'I found that pair of Claudia's. I'll bring them over to you later.'

We found the shop behind a square with super-posh houses built round a park-type garden blooming with magnolia trees.

'Bet it costs a packet to live here,' said Izzie, staring in the window of one of the houses next to the riding shop. The room looked like a film set with oak-panelled walls, old paintings and heavy red curtains.

The smell of leather hit us as soon as we entered the shop. It was crammed from floor to ceiling with everything you could imagine to do with horses – riding gear, boots, hats, stirrups, saddles, reins, books, magazines.

What I really wanted was one of the tweedy riding jackets but as I scanned the rails, I soon discovered that they were way out of my price range at over two hundred pounds. I was about to try one on to see what it looked like, when the door chimed open and I heard a voice I recognised. Luckily, we were at the back of the shop and hidden by rails full of clothes so she didn't see us.

'Hi,' said Cressida. 'I've come to pick up my outfit for next week's competition.'

'Miss Dudley-Smythe,' gushed the shop owner. 'How are you? And Lady Dudley-Smythe? Not with you today?'

I wasn't in the mood for bumping into WC. After having had such a nice day with the girls, I didn't want to ruin it.

'That's WC,' I whispered. 'I'm not up for saying hello. Let's try and get out without her seeing us.'

Of course Izzie wanted to have a peek at her, so she sauntered up to the front of one the aisles and pretended to have a look at some riding boots. She came back after a second.

'What's she doing?' I whispered.

'Chatting to the owners.'

'Can we sneak past?'

'Well, not all three of us,' said Izzie. 'But she doesn't know me and Lucy, so we could walk out easily. But what about you?'

She had another quick look at what was happening at the front of the shop. 'OK,' she said, coming back. 'This is the plan. They're on the right and look quite busy with clothes and stuff. So, Nesta, you walk to the left of us with your head turned away. Me and Lucy will be like a shield. Come on.'

We set off down the aisle nearest to the door with Lucy and Izzie on the right and me walking kind of sideways behind them. I had to bend my knees as I'm taller than both of them.

'Just go slow,' urged Izzie, 'kind of casual.'

As I half bounced, half slid along, I felt like John Cleese in the Monty Python programmes when he was doing the Ministry of Silly Walks. We'd almost made it to the door when Lucy got the giggles. She tried to hold it in but her shoulders began shaking up and down in silent laughter. That started Izzie off. Then, of course, me. Then Lucy couldn't hold it in a moment longer.

'Hooo, hoo HOOO,' she exploded.

The shop owners and Cressida looked around immediately.

'Nesta, is that you?' asked Cressida.

I was bent over the book section, heaving with laughter.

'Sneuck, yeah, bffff,' I said, trying to stop. 'Er, Cressida, this is Izzie and Lucy.'

'Hi, nnya, whey . . .' spluttered Izzie, who dove for the door quickly followed by Lucy.

'Do you know these girls?' said the shop owner, looking mystified by our behaviour.

'Yeah, sort of,' said Cressida disdainfully. 'What's so funny, Nesta?'

I coughed. 'Nothing. Er, private joke. Nothing.' I was just managing to get my face straight when I looked over Cressida's shoulder and out of the window.

Izzie and Lucy were outside pressing their faces up against the glass so that their features were all squashed. Both of them were doing mad faces and had made their eyes go cross-eyed.

I exploded laughing again.

'*Ummphh*. Gotta go, Cressida. See ya laters,' I stuttered.

As I ran for the door I could hear her saying, 'Honestly, some people are *so* juvenile.'

Nesta's Diary

Simon sent me loads of text messages today:

:-<   Missed U today.

I sent him back:

*^_^*   I had a good time with the girls.

He sent me back:

☹ because I wasn't there with U.

(He wants to meet Lucy and Iz so I hope WC doesn't

---

fill him in about bumping into us in the riding gear shop as I can just imagine her version.)

I sent him back:
:->>> because I'll see U in a few days.

Then he sent me this:
(*_*)

I had to text Izzie immediately to check it meant what I thought it did. It did. It does! It means I'm in love!!!!!

Treat 'em mean to keep 'em keen is my brother Tony's motto, or at least it was until he met Lucy who I still don't think he's quite got over. Anyway, I'm not going to be mean to Simon but I'm not going to tell him I love him back. Not yet. Even though I do.

Instead I sent him this: (OvO) It means I am a night owl.

He sent back ‹^O^› which means I am laughing loudly.

Me and the girls had a brill time today. Notting Hill is

the biz and I saw loads of things I wanted in the shops there. I felt a bit down about it after though, because our family is financially challenged at the moment. Tony came up with that term: he says it's a politically correct way of saying poor. He's mad. He's doing politics as one of his A levels and is always coming out with rubbish like that. Anyway, after feeling rotten about being financially challenged, I decided I ought to do something about it. Sink or swim time. I decided to swim and made A PLAN.

Chapter 6

Power Brekkie

The next morning, I got up early – well nine thirty, early for a weekend day – and checked my e-mails. I wanted to see if Lucy and Iz had replied to the invite I'd sent the night before:

```
Dear Ms Foster and Ms Lovering
Time: Sunday 10 a.m.
Place: Kitchen at Ms Williams's flat
Event: Power Breakfast.
Be there. Or be square.
Signed: Ms Nesta Williams. Esquire
HRH
```

Excellent. Both of them had replied that they'd come so I got dressed and went to buy the morning papers and croissants from the corner shop. When I got back, I began my preparations in the kitchen. Pens, writing pads, pencils, juice, fruit, tea, cereal, coffee, milk.

Then it was time to say hi to Mum.

I switched on the TV and flicked to the news station.

'Morning,' I said, as her face appeared on screen. Then I changed channels to MTV. My favourite band was on. Most excellent, I thought. I closed the kitchen door as I didn't want the music to wake Tony who was still in bed.

Lucy arrived first.

'I brought some blueberry muffins,' she said, handing over a bag. 'What's so important we have to get out of bed for?'

'I'll tell you when Iz arrives. Now. Orange juice, tea or coffee?'

'Juice,' said Lucy, looking at me suspiciously.

'What? *What?*' I laughed.

'You're up to something . . .'

Just at that moment, the doorbell rang.

'Lerrus in,' came Izzie's voice through the letterbox.

I went out into the hallway, knelt down and yelled back through the letterbox. 'Only if you know the secret password.'

Izzie started posting bananas through the door. 'Bananas,' she called. I love Izzie but there's no doubt, she is a Strange Friend.

I opened the door and burst out laughing. Izzie was

wearing jeans and a purple T-shirt, but she was also wearing the most enormous pair of knobbly shoulder pads, which made her look like an American football player.

'Power breakfast needs power dressing,' she laughed as she took two oranges out of her T-shirt and handed them to me along with a carrier bag. 'Needs *big* shoulders.'

'What are you like?' I laughed as I looked in the bag.

'Claudia's jodhpurs,' said Izzie.

'Cool. Thanks. I'll try them later.'

'So what's all this about?' she said, following me through to the kitchen.

'I read this article last night,' I explained, 'in one of Mum's magazines. It was about what businessmen do to begin their day. A power breakfast. It gets them revved up to go out and do their best.'

'Like motivates them?' asked Lucy, who had made a start on the croissants.

'Yeah.'

'But this is the Easter holidays, Nesta,' said Izzie, sitting at the breakfast bar and biting into one of Lucy's muffins. 'What's to get motivated for? It's time for . . .' she went into her American accent, 'rest and recuperation.'

'Only for slackers,' I said. 'High achievers never rest. They only stop for power breakfasts.'

'Yeah but at six a.m.,' remarked Lucy, looking at her watch, 'not ten fifteen after a lie-in.'

'Ah well. It *is* Sunday.'

'So why?' said Izzie. '*Why* am I here when I could have been tucked up under my duvet for at least another half hour?'

I picked up Mum's copy of *Woman Today* and read the list. 'Define goals. Identify negativity. Prioritise needs. And make up a game plan.'

'Oh,' said Lucy. 'That all?'

'Sounds impressive,' said Izzie.

'Yeah,' I said. 'Cool huh? It was just that when I got home last night I started feeling a bit of in-built free-floating depression . . .'

Izzie creased up laughing. 'Some *what*?'

'In-built free-floating depression . . .' I repeated. That was the term used in the article I'd read for when people couldn't get what they wanted and felt bad about it.

Izzie shook her head and gave Lucy one of her 'Nesta's a nutter' looks. 'What're you like?' she said. 'Everyone else gets a bit low from time to time. Oh, but not Nesta. Nesta has in-built free-floating depression.'

'Go on, laugh. Mock. I thought that you, of all people, would understand. I *do* have days when I'm down, you know.'

'Sorry, Nesta. I didn't mean to mock. You know that. It's just it . . .' she started sniggering again, 'it *is* a bit of a fancy term.'

'Everybody has their grey days, even me. And that's what got me thinking. You can either go down and be miserable or fight.'

'Sink or swim,' said Lucy.

'Yeah. I reckon that's what life is all about. Choices. You can go for what you want or watch everybody else get it and feel rotten.'

'Yeah,' said Lucy. 'She's right, Izzie.'

'You have to really focus on what you want,' I said.

'That's true,' said Izzie thoughtfully. 'All those wannabe popstars on telly now, some of them have been going at it for years.'

'Yeah. So I thought we could have our power breakfast and talk about strategy, game plans . . .'

'But first breakfast,' said Lucy eagerly. 'Shall I put the kettle on?'

'And I'll squeeze some fresh orange juice,' said Izzie.

At that moment, Tony staggered in in his usual morning disarray. He was half asleep and only wearing his boxer shorts. He woke up quickly when he saw Lucy.

'Hi, oh, whoops,' he said, covering his crotch with his hands and sort of dancing backwards out of the room. '*Nesta*. Why didn't you *tell* me you had guests?'

Hysterical, I thought. It really was. Tony was usually Mr Cool but he had a real thing about Lucy. I think it's because she's the only girl who's ever dumped him. And what a turn around, from her being all shy and in awe of him when she first met him – now she calls the shots. He's all gaga and she's all, Oh hi, Tony, you want to go on a date? Yeah . . . maybe. I'll call you sometime.

'You still cool about him these days, Luce?' I asked.

'Yeah. *Très* cool. I mean, he'll always be a bit special to me having been my first snog and that, but that's all.'

'Doesn't look like he's very cool,' remarked Izzie. 'In fact, I think he still fancies you.'

'Good,' smiled Lucy. 'It's nice to be admired. I just don't want to get into a heavy relationship at the moment. Now, who wants what?'

'You have learnt well, oh Lucy Skywalker,' I said, doing my Obi-Wan Kenobi voice. She has. Lucy used to be mega-uncool about boys, thinking she was lucky if one even looked at her. But she's got so much more confident in the last few months and now knows she doesn't have to say yes to the first one who looks her way. She's learnt the golden rule: boys run from desperate but run towards cool.

We spent the next half hour stuffing ourselves with toast and peanut butter and honey and cappuccinos made on Dad's machine. Then it was time to begin.

'So,' I said, wiping the last crumbs from the breakfast bar surface. 'The game plan. We each make our own. We have to write down the top three things we'd really like to achieve. Then what's holding us back.'

I pointed to the pens and paper I'd set out.

'Achieve like when?' asked Lucy. 'In the next few weeks or ten years?'

'Either or both. You can choose.'

Izzie chuckled. 'OK,' she said. 'Give us a pen.'

I scribbled my ideas quickly:

1) Be an actress (future)
2) Have lots of money (now)
3) Be very popular with everyone (now and future)

'I think we should be very specific,' said Izzie. 'You know, like, with details. Like if you're going to write – I want a boy to fall in love with me – you should specify that it's a decent-looking boy with a good personality or else you may get a boy to fall in love with you but he'll be a total plonker with knobbly knees and spots. Then we should put these notes in a secret wish box in a special place in our bedrooms.'

'Right,' me and Lucy chorused.

I added 'earning at least ten million a picture' to number one on my list and smiled to myself. I *knew* Izzie would get going in the end. In fact, she's usually the one who starts things like this. She's into all sorts of alternative therapies and self-help books and Lucy told me that she's even tried some witchcraft spells.

'Right, ready,' said Izzie after ten minutes.

'Yep, so am I,' said Lucy.

'OK, you go first, Izzie,' I said.

'One,' read Izzie, 'be a very successful and popular singer-songwriter. Two, get my own fabulous three-bedroomed flat – that's so you two can stay over. Three, travel the world first class and stay in fab locations.'

'OK,' I said. 'Lucy?'

'One. Career goal. Be a dress designer, successful. Two. Love goal. Meet my soulmate before I'm thirty. Fall in love with each other. Three. Home goal. To have a cottage in the country with dogs and cats and lots of animals.'

I quickly read mine then said, 'Right, now part two. The next thing to think about is how are you going to achieve this and what's holding you back.'

After another ten minutes of scribbling, we'd finished.

'I'll go first this time,' I said. 'OK. To get lots of money. Only solution is to get a job.'

'I thought you said babysitting didn't pay enough?' said Lucy.

'Doesn't.' I indicated all my newspapers on a chair by the door. 'I'm getting a proper job.'

'Have you found anything?' asked Lucy.

'I'm going to look later.'

'And what about the "being popular" bit?' asked Izzie.

'Easy. Just carry on being my natural charming self.'

'And modesty is your middle name,' laughed Izzie.

'So what's holding you back, then?' said Lucy. 'Sounds like you've got it all sorted.'

'I know what I want, but some days, with the acting bit, it's hard. I look at myself and think, what makes you so special? There are thousands of people out there all trying to make it.'

'My mum says there are two mistakes you can make in life,' said Lucy. 'The first is to think you're special. The other is to think that you're not.'

'Good quote,' said Izzie. 'But, Nesta, I'm sure you'd be a fabulous actress, and you're easily the best-looking girl in our school. All the boys swarm round you like bees round a honeypot. I wouldn't worry. Everybody has days when they doubt themselves. Days when they,' she grinned, 'feel in-built free-floating depression. You have nothing to worry about – you stand out in a crowd. People always do double-takes when they see you.'

'Yeah,' I said. 'But is that because they think I'm pretty or because I'm mixed race?'

'What difference would that make?' said Izzie, looking surprised.

'It's because you're pretty,' said Lucy. 'Course it is.'

'I'm not so sure,' I said. 'That's probably why a part of

71

me wants the right gear, you know, to fit in.'

'*Course* you fit in,' said Izzie. 'Doesn't matter what you wear.'

'I remember once when I was little,' I said. 'I was with my mum away for a weekend by the sea. Dad had gone off to get some ice creams and me and Mum were walking along the pier. This man passed us and did a double-take. He was really staring, then he came up to Mum and said, "Oi you, go back to your own country." He definitely wasn't staring because we were pretty. To him, we didn't fit in.'

'You're kidding?' said Izzie angrily. 'Where was this? Would you know him again if you saw him? I'll give him a piece of my mind. What was his name? How *dare* he?'

I had to laugh. Izzie looked like she was about to get on the next bus, go and find the man and challenge him to a fight. 'It was years ago, Iz. Mum told me to close my ears. But it was after that I noticed people staring at Mum. And staring at me.'

'I *hate* that,' said Izzie. 'More than anything. I can't stand people that are racist. It's so narrow-minded. It's what you're like on the inside that counts.'

'I think more often than not,' said Lucy, 'people stare at both you and your mum because you're both so glam. Not because of the colour of your skin.'

'Maybe,' I said, 'but I'll never know, will I? I remember

72

another day when I was about six, at school, there was a kid in the playground talking about coloured people. I remember thinking, how wonderful – a coloured person: purple legs, a green face, turquoise arms. I wanted to paint one in art. But then the kids started sniggering and pointing to me, saying that I was one. I hadn't really realised I was different until then. Then later, that man by the seaside – I decided no one was ever going to see if they had upset me. That's why I act confident. It doesn't mean I always am. I've just got good at the act.'

'I feel a bit like that with my height,' said Lucy. 'I know people think I'm just a kid because I'm so small. But, small, tall, fat, thin, black, white, you can't judge what people are like only by their appearance.'

'Well said,' said Izzie. 'We all have our hang-ups. And there will always be people who'll judge us.'

'What's your hang-up, then?' I asked.

'It's *exactly* what's getting in the way of me achieving what I want.'

'What do you mean?' asked Lucy.

Izzie looked worried. 'Well, you know Ben's been putting some of my lyrics to music?'

We both nodded.

'Well,' she continued, 'he's asked if I'll sing at the next gig with his band.'

'OhmyGod,' said Lucy. 'How brillopad is that? When?'

'Next week. Friday. But that's it. I don't mind singing in front of Ben. But at the thought of performing in public, I go cold. What if I dry up on the night? Just stand there with my mouth open and no words coming out? I'll look such a fool. I have nightmares about it.'

'Do what I do,' I said. 'On days I don't feel brave, I pretend I'm a character in a film and I think, OK, what would she do?'

'Oh God,' laughed Izzie, clamping her hands over her ears. 'You're going to sing that song from *The Sound of Music*. The one sung by Mother Superior. "Climb Every Mountain". Any minute. Aggghhh. Tell me when it's over.'

'I am not! And what a cheek,' I said, punching Izzie's arm. 'Nuns, I *don't* do.'

'Yeah, we'll be 'aving nun of that! But it's a good idea to think of a character,' said Lucy. 'It doesn't even have to be a film, does it, Nesta? She could just pretend to be some singer.'

'Who's the most confident singer you can think of?' I asked.

'Um, Madonna, I guess.'

'Right,' I said. 'Pretend you're Madonna.'

'And,' said Lucy, 'there's no time like the present. You can start by singing in front of us.'

'Oh no, *no*, I couldn't.'

Lucy put a tea towel on her head like a nun's wimple, joined her hands in prayer and started singing, completely out of key, 'Climb every mountain, ford every stream, er . . . follow every rainbow trout till you find your dream . . .'

'Aggggh,' said Izzie, putting her hands over her ears again. 'I give in. Mercy. Mercy.'

'If you can't sing in front of us, your best mates,' I said, 'you'll never do it. Now go outside and take a deep breath. Imagine Madonna in your head. Madonna who's going to sing one of your songs the best she's ever done.'

'Do I *have* to?' said Izzie.

'YES!' said me and Lucy.

'Or else I'll sing again,' said Lucy.

Izzie sighed and got down off her stool. 'Bossy pair. But I guess it is now or never.'

She went outside then returned a moment later.

'Can I sing facing the window?' she said.

'If that's how Madonna would do it, sure,' I said.

'Yeah, she's feeling a bit shy today,' said Izzie as she turned away from us. 'It's a song I wrote about stage fright.'

There was a moment's silence, then she started singing.

You say I got what it takes
And you say I know what makes the world go round,

But I don't know what I'm going to do about you.
I still can't go on.
You say I should leave the shadows
And run for the sun,
Stand in the spotlight and have some fun.
Your faith is my strength but I'm afraid I'll still fall.'

Lucy and I started cheering madly as Izzie turned round and bowed. She was good, really good. A deep velvety voice. Assured.

'Izzie, I never knew you could sing like that,' I said. 'That was really top.'

'Yeah,' said Lucy. 'With a voice like that, you've got nothing to worry about.'

'You think so?' she said, blushing red.

'Who was that singing?' said Tony, poking his head round the corner. He was dressed in his best pulling outfit. Black jeans and black T-shirt and he had his hair slicked back and reeked of Dad's Armani aftershave. It was so obvious he'd done it to impress Lucy. Poor boy. He's really got it bad.

'Our knight in shining Armani,' I laughed as he came in.

'It was Izzie,' said Lucy.

'Wow,' he said, looking at her with admiration. 'You've got a good voice.'

Izzie looked really chuffed. 'Thanks. And thanks, Nesta.

This power brekkie was a brillopad idea. Now, where are those papers? Let's find *you* a job.'

We spent the next hour looking for jobs for me but soon discovered I am unemployable. There's not a lot around for fourteen-year-olds.

There were jobs for drivers, but I can't drive.

Household interviewers, but car essential.

Cleaners needed, but have to have references. I doubt if Mum would give me one as it's not my best skill.

And finally, jobs for receptionists, but only the over-fifties need apply.

'There's nothing in here for you, Nesta,' said Izzie as she put the last paper down. 'You found anything?'

'Almost finished,' I said. I was looking through a local paper and something had caught my eye.

Earn between £100–£1000 a day as a full-time
or part-time model.

I jotted down the number on a bit of paper. £100–£1000 a day? I could help Mum and Dad out on that kind of money. Do it full-time in the holidays and part-time when I was at school. Hurrah! A solution.

I was about to tell the girls but Tony kept popping in, pretending that he needed stuff in the kitchen. It was *so* transparent that he wanted to be near Lucy. I decided not to say anything about the ad to the girls while he was there as he knew what Mum and Dad had already said about me modelling – that I couldn't even think about it until I had finished school.

I was dying to ask the girls what they thought, but Tone wouldn't go away. He kept asking if we wanted cappuccinos or toast or a bagel. Iz and I kept saying thanks, no and no, thanks. Lucy, on the other hand, was acting as if he wasn't even there.

Finally though, I think he'd had enough. He came and stood right in front of her and grinned cheekily.

'I suppose a snog's out of the question?' he asked.

Even Lucy couldn't resist that and she burst out laughing.

Nesta's Diary

☺ ☹ ☺ ☹ (An up and down day)

Major disaster after a good start. Discovered I am unemployable. ☹ ☹ ☹

Then I found a solution!!! ☺ ☺ ☺

Then I realised I was missing Simon so I messaged him:

RsQMe :-[[[[(rescue me, I am unhappy)

He wrote back IRLEWan2CU

So I sent :-D))(I'm very happy)

Then he sent :-)~ (I am drooling)

I sent (O-O) (I am shocked)

He sent (((H))) (a big hug)

So I sent <3 (love heart)

I know it's not exactly poetry, but then this is the 21st century.

My power breakfast was excellent. Iz sang in front of us and was really fab. She's got something special. Her and Lucy are top friends

Then I saw an ad for a model agency. People always tell me that I look like a model so I'm going to phone and check it out tomorrow.

Hurrah! Hurrah! ☺ ☺ ☺

Soon I will be wearing Gucci and earning loadsa£££££!

Chapter 7

Trustafarians

First thing the next day, I picked up the phone and dialled the number of the agency I'd seen in the paper.

'Morgan Elliot models,' said a voice at the other end.

'Good morgan, I mean morning,' I said, putting on my professional voice. 'I read your ad in the paper for models and wanted to know what to do next.'

'How old are you?'

I crossed my fingers. 'Sixteen,' I fibbed.

'Well, first you need to come in and let us see if you have potential, then, if we think you do, you have to register. That costs sixty pounds and you should bring two hundred pounds for your portfolio as we'll need pictures of you to send out to clients and we want to make you look the best you can. Now, would you like to arrange a time to come in and see Mr Elliot?'

Two hundred and sixty pounds? I thought. Where was

I going to get *that* from? I only had thirty pounds left in my savings. Maybe I could borrow some.

'Er, I'll think it over,' I said. 'I've had a few offers and want to consider my options.'

'What offers?' called Tony from the sitting-room.

'Er, none,' I said, putting down the phone and hoping that he hadn't overheard everything I'd said. 'Just going horse-riding again this afternoon, maybe . . . probably . . . that's one of my options.'

'With the trustafarians?'

'Durrhhh? The *what*?'

'Trustafarians. You know, kids whose parents put lots of dosh in trust for them, until they're twenty-one or something.'

'Oh, yeah, with them.'

'Down Hyde Park again?'

'Yeah,' I said, going in to join him on the sofa where he was watching a DVD of *The Matrix* for the third time.

'Can I come with you?' he said, flicking off the TV. 'I'm not doing anything and I'm *soooo* bored. All my mates have gone down the West End but . . . you know, with us being financially challenged . . . no dosh for Tone to play with. A day out on the horses sounds a laugh.'

Simon was cool about Tony coming too. As we made our way over to Kensington, he called on my mobile to say he'd meet us in the park as he was giving a little boy a lesson there before seeing us.

I spotted Simon waiting on the track by Alexandra Gate as soon as we arrived in the park. He had three horses with him and I felt myself smile inside as we got closer. Looking gorgeous in jeans and a Barbour jacket, he seemed to get better-looking every time I saw him.

'Hi,' he said, striding forward and shaking Tony's hand. 'You must be Nesta's brother?'

Tony grinned, nodded and pointed to the horses. 'One of these for me?'

'Certainly,' said Simon. 'Nesta said you'd never ridden before so I thought you might like to have a go. Here, put these on.'

As he handed us riding hats, the Portobello Princesses cantered by. WC was wearing her usual sour expression and was about to ride on. But then she saw Tony. I could see her say something to Tanya, then the two of them turned round, rode up to us and dismounted.

Off came her riding hat, *out* came her hair band as she shook her blonde hair and flicked it back, looking up at Tony flirtatiously. 'It's just *so* constricting,' she said, smiling widely at him, 'wearing your hair back all the time.'

I had to laugh to myself as I've seen girls react to Tony like this a million times.

Tony ran his fingers through his hair and kind of shook

his head like in a shampoo commercial. 'Ooooh. I know just what you mean . . .' he grinned back at her, giving her his killer charm look.

She snorted with laughter. Woah Neddie, I thought. He's not *that* funny.

'Cressida, Tanya, this is Nesta's brother, Tony,' said Simon.

As always, when Tony's introduced as my brother, the girls looked puzzled.

'Same dad, different mothers,' I said, going into the old familiar routine to explain our different colour skins.

'Oh, yah,' said Cressida, swishing her hair around, flick, flick, and not taking her eyes off Tony. 'My parents are divorced as well.'

'His mum's dead, actually,' I said flatly. How dare she assume that they'd got divorced?

Instead of looking embarrassed, WC linked her arm through Tony's. 'Oh, you poor darling,' she cooed. 'So you need a bit of looking after.'

'Yeah,' said Tony, who was loving every minute of it. 'So Cress,' he said. 'Gonna show me how to horse-ride?'

Cress(!!!?) giggled.

'It's his first time,' said Simon. 'Put him on Heddie.'

'Yes, my first time,' whispered Tony seductively and looking at Cressida meaningfully. 'I hope you'll be gentle with me.'

She shrieked with laughter again, then turned to Simon. 'Oh, don't put him on Heddie, Si. Let him go on Prince. I promise I'll take care of him.'

'Well I was going to put Nesta on Prince this time, but . . .'

'Oh, I don't mind,' I said. 'I don't mind Heddie. At least I know him from last time.'

As Tanya led the grey horse over to Tony, Cressida looked over at me and made eye contact for the first time.

Like *yeah*, I thought, I *am* here too.

The 'smell under her nose' look returned as she saw what I was wearing. '*Cream* jodhpurs!' she snorted. 'Nesta darling, *no one* wears cream jodhpurs.'

Luckily for her, Tony didn't hear as he was chatting to Tanya. Tony can be a flirt, but he's still my big brother and won't let anyone bully me or be horrid.

'Er, no, Cress *darling*, I think I do,' I said, smoothing the jodhpurs over my thighs. 'Not the sharpest knife in the drawer, are you?'

'No, really, sweetheart, it's you who's not the brightest crayon in the box,' cooed Cressida. 'Proper riders wear *dark* colours.'

I leant forward so only she could hear me. 'Actually, Cressida, most people wear dark colours to disguise their fat thighs. Very few people can wear cream. You have to be very slim to get away with it.'

She blushed angrily. I knew I'd hit a sore spot. She may have fabulous hair and a pretty face when she lightens up and she may be slimmish but her build is pear-shape, with a slightly big bottom and thighs.

I went over to join the others. I noticed Cressida hadn't said anything about Tony not wearing the right gear. He was dressed in khaki combats and a fleece, but Cressida didn't seem bothered about what he was dressed in, only that he paid her some attention. Tony was trying to get up on the horse and, a bit like me when I tried the other day, he was all over the place.

Cressida was straight in to help.

'Put your hand on my shoulder,' she said, diving in beside him. 'Foot in the stirrup, then lift yourself up.'

Tony milked it for all he was worth. First he managed to get his foot stuck in the stirrup so he had to hang on to Cressida to hold him up. Unlike my first time when she'd laughed at me, this time she was all kindness and understanding.

Luckily for Tony, Prince was a patient horse and didn't seem to mind his antics as he attempted to get up into the saddle but kept falling back into Cressida's waiting arms. Hah, I thought. If only you knew what he was really like. Tony's one of those rare boys who can fool girls into thinking she's the only one there and *so* special. I'd seen him do it so many times. He may be gorgeous to look at but I know what a love rat he really is.

Simon helped me up on to Heddie and when we were all ready, we began to trot up the track. Cressida gave me a filthy look as she passed me so I grinned back at her and turned my riding hat round backwards like some people wear their baseball caps.

'You have to wear the proper gear to be a serious rider,' I called to Tony who was behind me. He gave me the thumbs-up and promptly turned his hat round backwards as well.

Simon cracked up and immediately did the same.

Cressida turned back and was about to scowl when she saw what I had done. Then she saw Tony and Simon's hats and looked like she was going to be sick as she tried to change the scowl to a smile.

'Cool, huh, Cress?' called Tony.

'Er, yah,' she said. But she couldn't bring herself to turn her hat round.

Nesta's Diary

Had a brillopad day riding today. Looked fab in cream jodhpurs. WC was sniffy about them. Later on Simon explained that serious riders only wear dark jodhpurs because they have to muck out their horse's stable after riding. Poo. I can't imagine owning my own horse. Must be top.

It was cool having Tony along today. WC made an effort to be more pleasant to me because he was there. Well, at least when he was around. Must make use of this and take him along more often. We had a real laugh wearing our hats backwards but of course WC was suffering her usual sense of humour failure and was not amused.

Phoned model agency. They want £260 to register and do a portfolio. Am seriously considering it so that I can be mega-rich and buy a whole stable of horses.

Am getting the hang of horse-riding. Be cool. Be unafraid. Be gentle. Don't try and run before you can walk. Ha ha.

I got on a lot better with Heddie today. I didn't feel so frightened and I think the feeling was mutual.

I don't think it must be very nice to have a leathery bit thing in the mouth that people pull on. No wonder he wouldn't do what I wanted the first time, when he wanted to eat grass and I kept yanking him up. It must have hurt. Now I have decided to be very gentle and just nudge him a little when I want to go off instead of kicking him. It seemed to work better. I think he knew I was trying to be nice. Also, it's common sense that if you treat anyone, human or animal, nicely, they will be nice back (except WC).

Maybe if I don't become an actress I will be the English Horse Whisperer. Maybe not, as that would probably mean mucking out, which I don't fancy the sound of at all.

Chapter 8

Strange but Healthy Meal

Sometimes holidays can seem like eternity, I thought, as I mooched around our empty flat the following morning. All the world seemed to be busy except me.

Simon was going to lunch with his dad at a hotel called the Connaught. They were going to discuss His Future.

Izzie was rehearsing with Ben the Buddhist and his band King Noz. She'd decided at the power breakfast that she's going to go for it and sing at the next gig. It's a really big deal for her as she's never shown anyone her songs, never mind performed live in front of an audience. She is very brave.

Lucy was being all secretive and said she was doing a 'sewing project'.

Tony had gone to Hampstead Heath with yet another

girlfriend. He's been going through them like hot cakes lately. One a week. The phone's always going with girls on the other end wanting to speak to him. He says it's the only way to help him get over Lucy. I know he's hoping that I'll pass this on and make Lucy jealous, but I don't. Lucy seems to be doing just fine without him, unlike some other girl I could name. It was hysterical when we went horse-riding – Cressida was all over him like a rash and dropped humungous hints that she didn't have a boyfriend at the moment and was free in the week. But Tony was doing his cooler than cool act and didn't ask her out. He said he prefers Tanya anyway.

Mum was working the sunrise shift again. She still hasn't heard if her contract was to be renewed and has been spending loads of time these days scouring newspapers looking for alternative jobs.

Dad wasn't due back from Manchester until Friday night. I'll probably be in bed when he arrives. I'll leave a nice welcome home note for him.

And me? Not busy. Unoccupied.

I picked up the papers I'd bought a couple of days before and was about to put them in the recycling bin. Should I try the modelling agency again, I wondered? Maybe I could just go down there and check the place out? I wouldn't have to commit. Should I? Shouldn't I?

I picked up the telephone and dialled.

'Can I come over?' I asked when Lucy answered the phone. 'I know you're sewing but I promise I'll sit in the corner and won't make a sound. You won't even know I'm there.'

'Sure,' said Lucy. 'In *fact*, I may have a surprise for you.'

Lucy's bedroom floor was knee-deep in bits of assorted fabric.

'Careful,' she said from her desk where she was sitting in front of her mum's sewing machine. 'Stand on the bits of carpet in between.'

'What are you making?' I said as I tiptoed my way through bits of lace, silk and crêpe to the bed.

'I'm experimenting. See,' she pointed to a newspaper by her bed, 'have a look in there. A few pages in. I nicked it from one of your papers on Sunday. Look at the page about fashion week. There's a designer called Elspeth Gibson, got it? Read what it says about her.'

I turned to the page she said and scanned the many designers featured on the page: Ben de Lisi, Ronit Zilkha, Ghost, then in the bottom right, Elspeth Gibson.

'Wow. Lucy. These are lush,' I said, looking at the designs.

'Yeah, but read what it says about Elspeth Gibson,' insisted Lucy.

'Jodhpurs are topped with fragile Edwardian-style

blouses and a hacking jacket goes over a flirt's skirt of frothy chiffon . . .'

'Exactly,' interrupted Lucy, indicating the floor with her arms. 'We've got frothy, we've got chiffon. It says what's in is a mixture of new and vintage. Like tweed with organza, a bit of lace against chiffon, velvet and Lycra.'

'You're really into all this, aren't you?' I asked. She looked so animated. Enthusiastic.

Lucy nodded. 'I've really found my thing. I love making clothes. And seeing those designs in the paper, I thought that's exactly what I like doing. Mixing old and new. Vintage clothing is still in. Loads of celebs wear it for the Oscars.' She pointed to the wardrobe. 'Have a look in there, Nesta, at the bottom.'

I did as I was told, being careful not to stand on the bits of material on the floor. I reached into the wardrobe and pulled out the bin bag. It was full of bits of material and old clothes.

'What am I looking for?' I asked, sifting through more cut-up blouses on the top.

'A jacket down the bottom somewhere. That's the bag of stuff that belonged to my grandmother.'

'Ah,' I said. 'The treasure trove.'

I knew all about this bag. In the autumn term, Lucy had found it in the cupboard under the stairs where her mum had stashed it years ago with a load of junk. It was full of clothes from the forties and fifties. Lucy used bits of the old fabric to do some of her early designs, two of which were fab tops for Izzie and me.

'It's at the bottom,' said Lucy, watching me rummage around.

In the end, I emptied all the clothes out on the floor, adding to the mess.

'There,' said Lucy, pointing to a jacket.

I picked it up. 'OhmyGod.'

'Try it on,' beamed Lucy.

It was the most perfect riding jacket.

'I know,' grinned Lucy. 'It was after we'd been to that riding gear shop the other day. I thought, I'm *sure* I've seen a jacket like that somewhere, but I didn't say at the time as I didn't want to get your hopes up.'

The label inside said *Harris Tweed* and it was brown with little fudge- and cream-coloured flecks. It was far nicer than any of the ones we'd seen in the shop. I put it on. It fitted perfectly and was beautifully cut, nipping in at the waist.

'Sleeves are a bit short,' said Lucy, getting up and examining the arms, 'but I can let them down a little.'

'Lucy, I *love* it. Can I wear it? Really?'

'Yeah, course, it's yours,' said Lucy. 'And that's not all.' She held up a floaty cream voile blouse with a ruffle down the front.

'Try it on with this,' she said. 'I made it from that dress that I got from Portobello.'

'But you bought it for you,' I said. 'For the material.'

'Loads of material left in the skirt,' said Lucy. 'And, anyway, all good designers have models that take their collections out into the public. You can be my live mannequin. Come on, try it on.'

I stripped off and put on the blouse, then the jacket.

'Wear those with your cream jodhpurs and I reckon you'll look like you stepped straight out of *Vogue.*'

I looked at my reflection in the mirror. She was right. The outfit looked just like one of those from the fashion week.

'And if I borrow Mum's knee-high boots, it'll look amazing,' I said. 'Lucy, you really are a top friend.'

Lucy blushed. 'No prob,' she said. 'Now let's let those sleeves down.'

After Lucy finished her sewing, I gave her a manicure and pedicure as a thank you. And I did it really properly. I got a bowl from the kitchen and filled it with hot water. Then we put in some of the magnolia bubble bath that Lucy got for Christmas and she soaked her feet. Then I did a bit of a massage on her feet and hands with vanilla body lotion before painting her nails the pale blue colour that she's into at the moment.

Around six o'clock, Izzie turned up from her rehearsal

and Lucy's mum said we could all stay and have supper if we didn't mind eating on our knees in front of the TV.

'I can't be bothered doing a big number at the table,' she said.

She's so cool is Mrs Lovering, really laid-back and easy.

I love being at their house. All of them have made me feel like one of the family ever since I arrived in London. *However* when it came to eating there, I wasn't so sure. They eat some very weird stuff at the Loverings'. Even Lucy would agree. Her dad runs the local health food shop and sells all the health foods that Izzie is into but I've never heard of.

After half an hour or so, Mrs Lovering brought through plates of food.

'Mmm, smells good,' said Izzie.

'What is it?' I asked.

'Quinoa, steamed vegetables and soya sauce,' said Mrs Lovering. 'And to make it a bit more interesting, I've chopped in some nori.'

Lucy and I exchanged looks.

'Mmm, my *favourite*,' I said as Lucy and I both burst out laughing. She knew I hadn't got a clue what quinoa or nori were.

Izzie raised her eyes to heaven. 'Nori is seaweed. And quinoa is like a grain. It's really good for you.'

I took a forkful and put it in my mouth as I do believe

in trying everything once. It tasted like rice mixed with freshly mown grass and lemon. 'Yeah. Suppose it's OK.'

'Yeah,' said Lucy, chewing a bit of hers then going into her best Shakespearian actor luvvie voice. 'But *ohhh* how I *lonnngggg* for egg and chips and *beeeeans* some *niiiights*.'

'How was rehearsal?' I asked Izzie after we'd finished our Strange But Healthy Meal.

'Tough,' she said. 'But fun. They're well pleased that I'm going to sing. At first I was soooo nervous, but then we went over and over it to the point where I just wanted to get it right and stopped thinking about my knocking knees.'

'What are you going to wear?' asked Lucy.

'Ah. Not sure. I had thought maybe my velvet . . .'

'Where's the gig?' I interrupted.

'Somewhere in Kentish Town.'

'Then *not* your velvet. It's too "nice girl who lives in Hampstead",' I said. 'You need to look dangerous, like you've got an edge.'

'That's exactly what Ben said,' said Izzie. 'In fact, he's working at this place his cousin owns in Camden Lock, just for the hols, to get some dosh so we can hire a studio to do a demo tape. He says he thinks I should go down there and have a look before deciding on anything.'

'If Ben's a Buddhist, he might kit you out in Eastern robes,' I said.

'Nah. He says this shop is mega, like nothing he's ever seen before.'

'When shall we all go?' said Lucy. 'Next week?'

'Yeah,' said Izzie. 'Brillopad. And you'll come to the gig as well, won't you? To see me sing?'

'Wouldn't miss it for the world,' said Lucy. 'But how are things with you and Ben apart from the singing?'

Izzie grinned. 'Most excellent. He's so cool and – oh, he says that there are some people coming to check out the band from a record agency. We need as many people there in the audience as possible, so it looks like the band's really popular.'

'I'll bring Simon and the Princesses,' I said. 'It's about time they came up to our neck of the woods.'

Chapter 9

Prada 'n' Prejudice

'Nesta! You look totally amazing,' said Tanya as she opened the door to their house in Holland Park. 'Where did you get that fab gear?'

'Oh, a little designer I know in North London,' I said casually as I stepped into a vast marble hallway.

Lucy *is* little. In fact, she's only four foot eight.

I knew I looked good. I'd spent ages getting ready as I'd decided to show Simon exactly how I could look if I tried. He'd only ever seen me in my scruffs. This time, I'd washed and conditioned my hair in camomile rinse so it looked really silky. Then I'd painted my nails with Mum's Chanel Rouge Noir. After that, I'd put on some Mac kohl and Bobbi Brown lipstick and a little blusher. Then on with my Lucy Lovering designer extraordinaire outfit – that is, the blouse and jacket were from Lucy but I wore them with a ra-ra skirt, not jodhpurs, as we weren't riding. I got the skirt at Christmas from Morgan; it's made of a bronze swishy material that flares out in a little frill just above my knees. Looked great with the blouse. And to complete it all, I'd borrowed a pair of Mum's sexy Jimmy Choos.

'I wish I could wear shoes like that,' said Tanya, 'but they kill my feet. You walk in them so easily.'

'Just takes practice,' I said. Hah! If only she'd seen me round the corner a few minutes ago. I'd worn my Nikes most of the way and changed into the killer heels at the last minute so I wouldn't have to walk far.

'Simon's in the library,' said Tanya. 'Come through.'

'With Miss Scarlet and the rope?' I joked as I took in the luxurious surroundings, but Tanya looked blank.

'Cluedo,' I explained. 'Have you never played it? Who did the murder? Professor Plum in the hall with the dagger or Mrs White in the library . . . oh never mind.'

I tried not to look too gobsmacked when Tanya opened the door to the library. There's serious money in these here walls, I thought, as I took in the airy elegant room. Heavy ivory silk curtains hung at windows that must have been at least ten metres high. Plush pale sofas were arranged opposite each other in front of the most stunning fireplace I have ever seen. It was white marble. A man's torso was carved out on each side with fruit and grapes and leaves winding round him. From floor to ceiling were shelves lined with endless books. Even the flower arrangement on the piano looked like it had cost a small fortune. No simple daffs for this household, here were lilies, white roses and orchids. Shame about the rugs though, I thought, as I walked over to the sofas. They were beautiful, but looked a bit faded round the edges.

Simon looked like he was asleep and Cressida was jabbering on her mobile phone while flicking through a copy of *Tatler* which lay on top of a pile of glossy magazines. *Country Life. Vogue. Harpers & Queen. Vanity Fair.*

'Nesta's here,' announced Tanya.

Cressida ignored me and turned her knees towards the fireplace whilst continuing her phone conversation. Simon opened his eyes, looked up sleepily, then his face lit up. 'I was just thinking about you,' he said, getting up to greet me. 'You look beautiful.' Then he turned to Tanya. 'Aren't you two off somewhere?'

'Yeah, yeah, ballet,' said Tanya. 'And I think I can safely guess what you two will be up to. Come on, Cressida, or we'll be late.'

Cressida gave me a cursory glance, then did a double-take and checked out my outfit. She raised her eyebrows slightly, but didn't say anything.

Some people find it hard to give compliments, I thought, and some people find it hard to receive them. Me, I'm good at both and decided maybe it was time she learnt from the Master.

'You're looking good today,' I said to Cressida as she picked up a little handbag from the coffee table. 'Cool bag.'

Before she could stop herself, she smiled. 'Thanks. It's Prada.'

Then, before I could stop myself, I blurted, 'Oh. Like in that book by Jane Austen?'

'What book?' asked Cressida, taking the bait like a dream.

'*Prada 'n' Prejudice*,' I said.

Simon and Tanya burst out laughing. 'Oh very good,' said Tanya. 'In fact, we're doing *Pride and Prejudice* at school next term.'

Cressida didn't laugh. I was waiting for one of her eyebrows to go up or down. She had quite a range of eyebrow expressions. Left one up for an 'I'm superior' look. Right one up for disdain. Both up for bored interest. Both down and pulled together for disapproval.

'Actually, before you go, I wanted to ask you both something,' I said.

They stopped at the door.

'My friend Izzie is singing at a gig on Friday night and I wanted to know if you'd like to go.'

'Yah, OK,' said Tanya. 'I don't think we're doing anything.'

'Is she one of the girls who was in the shop the other

day?' asked Cressida. Aley-oop. Eyebrow up.

'Yeah. Dark-haired one,' I said. 'She has an amazing voice and sings with a band called King Noz. They're getting a really good name for themselves round North London.'

'Well I'm in,' said Simon.

'Where exactly will this gig be?' drawled Cressida.

'Kentish Town somewhere. I'll let you know nearer the time.'

'*Kentish* Town? Where's that?' asked Cressida. Smell under nose and both eyebrows down.

Stuck-up cow, I thought. I was about to tell her that there is life outside West London but then I remembered Izzie wanted loads of people at the gig to impress the talent scouts.

Then inspiration struck. I *know* how to get you there, I thought.

'There's a whole crowd of us going,' I said. 'Lucy, her brothers, *Tony*.'

Suddenly Cressida looked interested, but I looked directly at Tanya. 'I know he'd like to see you again.'

Of course, Cressida thought I meant her.

'I suppose we could go,' she said. 'In fact, why not? It'll be a hoot.'

After they'd gone, I settled in with Simon on the sofa. Even though it was spring, there was a real fire burning and the atmosphere was so cosy I thought we could stay there all afternoon. It was the first time I'd been alone with him properly since I'd met him and I didn't fancy trawling round the pavements in Mum's shoes. They look good but they're clearly not for walking in.

'Shall we stay here?' I said, snuggling up to Simon.

He put his arm round me. 'Yeah. Mum's around somewhere. In fact, I want to introduce you but she's upstairs with one of the slave team in at the moment.'

'Slave team?'

'Yeah. She has a whole load of people who look after her.'

'Is she ill?'

Simon laughed. 'No. She's an interior designer. She's quite famous.' He indicated the fabulous flowers. 'Our home is her showcase so she has a florist who comes in to make sure the place looks good. A nutritionist to make sure she eats right. A manicurist and pedicurist to make sure her nails look good. A hairdresser . . . Then she has her PA and her reflexologist and her aromatherapist and beautician . . .'

'We also have people who come to the house,' I said. 'The milkman, the postman, the dustbin men . . .'

Simon laughed, but I felt sad for a minute because there was my mum worrying about work and money and telling us to economise and here was I sitting in this mega-posh place surrounded by dosh. Eight people to look after one! His mum must earn a fortune, I thought. Life's a funny business. Why are some people so rich and others have nothing? I must ask Izzie later. She's bound to have some kind of answer.

'I think Mum's having a massage,' said Simon, putting his arm around me, 'so that means she won't be around for a while.'

'Cool,' I said and took his other hand in mine.

Simon stroked my fingers and sort of massaged my palm. It was heavenly. Holding hands can be so nice if you do it properly I've discovered. Almost as good as kissing.

'Actually, I was going to ask you something,' he said when we came up for air after a divine snogathon. 'There's a whole gang of us going away next week, for a few days. Skiing. At Courchevel. There were six of us but my friend Marcus has dropped out and I wondered . . . do you think you might be able to come?'

'God, I'd love to . . .' I began but I realised this was the time to come clean. My family couldn't begin to keep up with his. No doubt about it, especially now that I had seen where he lived. Izzie's words of encouragement echoed in my mind and gave me the strength to say what I knew I must.

He likes you no matter what, she'd said.

I had to tell him I couldn't possibly ask my mum. It

wasn't only the trip away, there would be the gear to buy, and pocket money. Mum had enough stress as it was without me laying more on her. She'd been looking tired lately. And even Dad sounded strained when I talked to him on the phone. It's *them* that needed the holiday break, never mind me.

'You know what I really admire about you?' said Simon just as I opened my mouth to explain.

'What?'

Your amazing attitude. You don't let *anything* faze you. It's the kind of attitude that we're always being encouraged to have at school. Even my dad was on about it the other day at lunch. But *you* don't have to learn it. It's natural with you. You're one of life's winners. Other people give up before they've even begun but not you. You go for it.'

Gulp. How can I possibly tell him now? I thought. Shatter his illusions that I am a tip-top winner-type person? Tell him I can't go to Courchevel. That my family's broke?

Er. I don't *think* so.

Nesta's Diary

Très interesting day.

Simon's house is out of this world. Stunning. Classy. Going to the loo there is a spiritual experience as everything is so beautiful.

Lovely sandalwood soaps by Floris. Air freshener by Czech and Speake.

The sink and taps were a work of art.

I took notes of everything for when I am rich and famous.

Piles of white towels. Izzie's mum would think she'd died and gone to heaven (she's big on white towels as well).

Met Simon's mum briefly. She looks expensive. Blonde with not a hair out of place. Dressed in cashmere. Looks like she sweats French perfume.

Big dilemna though. I said I'd go to Courchevel. Tony told me it's a super fab ski resort and loads of the boys from his school go there.

V. expensive.

I thought again about contacting the model agency but even with them, I wouldn't have the money in time. So. I'm drawing out my £30 savings and I'm going to gamble. Scratchcards.

Chapter 10

Cyberdog

'You're mad,' said Izzie, when I met her on the corner of our road. 'Do you know what the chances are of you actually winning? It's like, millions to one.'

'So? Someone's got to win. Why not me?'

'But, why do we have to go to East Finchley High Road?'

'In case anyone sees us. I can't risk running into Mum or Tony or someone in Highgate.'

'Are we meeting Lucy?'

I shook my head. 'Nah. You have to be sixteen to buy Instant cards. Someone might suss that I'm not old enough if she was with us.'

'God, you've really got this all worked out, haven't you?'

'You bet,' I said, then laughed. 'I mean *I* bet.'

'Well as long as you know I don't approve,' said Izzie. 'And I did promise Lucy I'd take her with me to Cyberdog today.'

'Cyberdog?'

'The shop where Ben's working. The manager is his cousin. He said I could borrow an outfit for the gig as it will be publicity for the shop.'

'Cool. Maybe I could buy something there with my winnings. I've got thirty quid left in the world and I reckon that will give me a good chance.'

'OK,' she said doubtfully. 'But don't blame me if you lose it all.'

'I'm feeling lucky. And my horoscope said I may get a windfall this week.'

That shut her up. Izzie's *well* into astrology.

'It's like, sometimes in life, you have to gamble. Someone has to win. If you're not in, you can't win.'

'Yeah. Maybe. Whatever,' said Iz.

We came across a newsagent in the High Road with a Lottery sign outside and I quickly looked up and down the road to make sure that no one I knew was about. Like Mrs Allen the headmistress, or Tony.

I felt like a spy on a mission. 'Just call me Bond. James Bond. Double-oh-seven,' I said.

'You'll be more like double-oh-zero when you've no money left,' laughed Izzie.

'Coast clear,' I said as I opened the door and stepped inside.

Now. Which to choose? There were about eight varieties.

Now how much do I want to win? I thought. One thousand pounds. Five thousand pounds, twenty thousand, or the big one, one hundred thousand pounds.

'Are you going to get one of each?' asked Izzie, looking at the cards.

I shook my head. 'No. I read somewhere that they only put a winning card in every now and again so I reckon I have a better chance of winning if I buy a few of one type from the same roll.'

I decided to go for the big one.

'Can I have five of those Instant scratchcards?' I asked the Indian lady behind the counter. 'The ones for one hundred thousand.'

May as well aim high, I thought, as a thrill of anticipation ran through me.

'There may be more winners on the smaller amounts,' said Izzie, eyeing the chocolate on display.

'No. Final decision,' I said. As I handed over my money I spotted something I knew Izzie would like. 'Er, and a bar of Green and Blacks.'

I handed Izzie the bar of organic chocolate and we went and sat on a bench in the High Road outside Budgens. I pulled out my purse and got out a coin.

'What would you do if you won?' asked Izzie, popping a piece of chocolate in her mouth.

Ah, my favourite fantasy, I thought. 'I'd have a party

with all our friends . . . Buy some new clothes . . . Get a car . . .'

'But you can't drive yet.'

'Yeah, but for when I can. Then I'd get presents for you and Lucy and Tony and Mum and Dad. I'd go on holiday with you and Lucy. I'd take you to St Kitts in the Caribbean where Mum's from. You'd love it: sand like talcum powder and the colours are to die for — turquoise, aquamarine . . . gorgeous. Then to Ravello in Italy, where Dad was born. It's high on the Amalfi Coast. Amazing. Then I'd buy a flat. Get horse-riding lessons for Lucy and me. Buy you a studio . . .'

Izzie laughed. 'Er, Nesta . . . you'll only have *one* hundred thousand if you win . . .'

'Money makes money. Isn't your mum always saying that? Anyway . . . what would you do?'

'Travel. Goa. Los Angeles. Phuket. Save some. Get a band together and a demo CD. Stuff like that.'

I began scraping the cards. 'OK, here goes.'

First one. Nothing.

Second one and my heart began to beat as I saw £100,000 appear. Then *another* £100,000.

'OhmyGod . . .' I held my breath as I scraped off the rest of the card.

Then my heart sank. £6. £10. £25.

Ah well, three more cards to go.

I could see Izzie having to bite her tongue as I finished scraping the last one. She was dying to say, 'I told you so.'

I waved the last one in her face. 'I've *won*!!!'

'*Really*!' she gasped. 'How much?'

'A *pound*,' I said. 'Whoo*pee*. Let's go and collect our winnings.'

After we'd picked up the pound coin from the newsagents, we walked a bit further down to a garage. The man at the till hardly even glanced up at me so I bought ten cards. Once again, a thrill of anticipation ran through me. This was serious fun. It was really exciting as each time I got a handful of cards, I felt full of hope. Possibilities. Until I scratched the cards, there was a chance I might win. Change my life. Change Mum and Dad's lives.

We sat on the brick wall by the road and I scraped five and Izzie did five. This time I won two pounds. Never mind, I told myself, I still had fifteen pounds left.

'Oh, let's go,' said Izzie. 'You've lost half your money. I can't bear it. Maybe your horoscope was right, and you've got your windfall – three pounds. Let's buy some chips with the winnings and go and collect Lucy.'

There was *no way* I was giving up then. It was far too exciting and it wasn't over yet. And I hadn't lost *all* my money. Only half of it.

And I'd won three pounds.

And what *if*? What if I did give up and the *very* next card I was going to buy was the *one*? *The winning card*?

I couldn't back down now.

But which shop was the winning card in? The newsagents? The corner shop?

'Let's try the Post Office,' I said and set off eagerly.

'I'm going to Lucy's,' said Izzie. 'Are you coming with me?'

'No way,' I said. 'I'll only be another ten minutes. Why won't you stay?'

'Because this is a total waste of your money and it's painful to watch.'

Killjoy, I thought. There was no way I was going to stop now. I *had* to carry on. I couldn't even *think* about stopping.

'I'll meet you at Lucy's when I've finished,' I said. 'Be prepared to celebrate.'

'Yeah, whatever,' said Izzie, heading for the bus stop. 'Later.'

Honestly, I thought, as I puffed my way back up the High Road. She's got no sense of adventure, that girl.

I saw another sign for the Lottery outside the Post Office. I bet that's where the winning card is, I thought. I can just feel it in my bones. I was just about to go in when I saw one of our teachers, Miss Watkins, in the queue. I did a quick turn around. She was the last person I wanted to bump into.

I walked a bit further up and found a corner shop that sold scratchcards and there I bought seven. I decided to buy some of the ones with lesser prizes of two thousand five hundred, just in case Izzie had been right and you stood a better chance of winning.

I put them in my bag then went back to the Post Office.

I quickly checked that Miss Watkins had gone then, seeing that all was clear, I joined the queue. I was feeling really elated. I was sure the winning card was here.

An old woman in front of me bought some writing paper and when I saw she'd finished at the counter I stepped forward.

But then the woman turned back. She looked at the scratchcards. 'Oh go on,' she said to the lady behind the counter. 'I'll have three.' Then she saw me. 'Oh, sorry love,' she said. 'Do you want to go? I'm in no hurry.'

Oh *no*, I thought, panicking. *Decisions*. Should I let her have the next cards or should *I* buy them? Should I wait and let her go before me or should I butt in and take the next cards? What if the very next card is *The One* and I let her buy it? *Aaaghhhh*!

'No, you go ahead,' I said.

She bought her cards and I stepped forward again.

'Eight of the hundred thousand pound cards,' I said, laying my money out on the counter.

The lady behind the till smiled. 'Feeling lucky?' she asked as she ripped eight cards off the roll.

'Yeah,' I said. But I wasn't so sure any more.

On the bus to Lucy's, I sat at the back and got busy scraping the cards from the Post Office. One, two, three, four, five, six, seven, eight. Nothing. Not even a pound.

Then I got out the seven cards from the newsagent's. Maybe I'd have to settle for one of the smaller prizes. Scrape, scrape. One, two, three, four, five, six. Nothing.

The feeling of anticipation had now been replaced by disappointment. And horror. I'd spent all my money. I had nothing left to last me through the rest of the holidays.

I had one card left. I was about to start scraping but stopped myself and put it back in my purse for later. As long as I didn't look at it or scrape it, there was still a chance, some hope that it was a winner. I'd do it when I got to Lucy's.

But already there was a sinking feeling in the pit of my stomach. I had no money left at all now. That hadn't been part of the plan.

When I reached Lucy's, she took the card I handed her and scraped off the last bits of silver.

She looked up at me sadly. 'I *am* sorry, Nesta,' she said. 'Nothing.'

I sighed. 'Do you think I need to go to Gamblers Anonymous?' I asked. 'Now that I'm an addict.'

Izzie laughed. 'Not yet. But I do think that the only kind of Instant you should stick to in the future is the mashed potato variety.'

Lucy's dad dropped us in Camden. He drove us there in their hippie-dippie car and as always people stared at us when we drove by. The car does make quite a statement. It's an old Volkswagon Beetle and it's bright turquoise with a big lilac flower painted on the boot. No one batted an eyelid when we got to the Lock. The hippie-dippie look has come back in fashion there along with flares and tie-dye T-shirts.

'Ben says the shop is under the arches in the stable part of the market,' said Izzie, leading us through a gate behind the main market.

The courtyard was heaving with people who looked like they were either at a fancy dress party or a meeting of different tribespeople. There were skinheads, goths, hippies and punks. And wandering round in the middle, looking amazed by the sights, were little groups of tourists all dressed neatly in Benetton best. Music of every variety pounded out from different stalls: techno, Latin, garage, turbo, trance, hip-hop, sixties, seventies, heavy metal. Every way you turned there were sounds. And smells.

The delicious aroma of garlic, spices and onions hit us

as we pushed our way through the crowds.

'You like some noodles, pretty lady?' called a Thai girl from behind an enormous steaming wok.

'I'd give *anything* for noodles,' I said. 'But I have no money.'

The girl pulled a sad face, then called to a crowd of goth girls behind me.

'Wow,' I said, pulling Lucy's arm. 'Look, *look*, behind, a posse of death-cult zombie girls.'

Lucy giggled as a group of teenagers dressed in goth black drifted by. Their faces were plastered in white make-up and their hair was black with purple streaks and so lank it looked like it hadn't been washed. Ever.

'I can't imagine what there is here,' I whispered to Lucy. 'I mean, most people we've seen are either retro, goths or punks – nothing really new.'

'Ben says it's the most happening place in London at the moment,' said Izzie.

'And I'm hoping I can pick up some tips for my design work,' said Lucy. 'All the papers say that what's happening is vintage mixed with new. I need to check out if that's right.'

The seductive smell of caramel hit my nostrils as we passed a stall selling roasted nuts. I groaned. 'Oh. I'm hungry,' I wailed.

Izzie raised an eyebrow. 'You've only yourself to blame,' she said.

I stuck my tongue out at her back as I hurried along behind her into a passageway. Soon the smell of food was replaced by a strong smell of joss-sticks.

Loud music was pulsating from an entrance under one of the arches in a corner.

'Here it is,' said Izzie, pointing up to the sign 'Cyberdog'.

As we stepped inside, the music was throbbing and the ground shaking with the base.

It was like we'd walked into a spaceship. Brick walls were painted silver, orange and turquoise. Perspex tables lined the walls where people were seated playing on iMac computers and sipping cappuccinos. Dry ice was being pumped up from the floor, giving the place an other-worldly look.

Izzie disappeared off to look for Ben and Lucy and I went through an archway into what looked like a clothes shop.

The clothes on the rails looked like they'd been stolen from the set of Star Trek. One top was made of rows of red Perspex, the ridges made to look like ribs. And the shop assistants looked like alien mutants. They were all dancing wildly to the music.

Lucy and I stood and stared. One girl in front of me had her head shaved except for a pink fluorescent ponytail at the back. She was wearing head-to-foot canary yellow. On her calves she had huge yellow furry leggings. Through her earlobes, she had about twelve rings, a stud through her nose and another through her mouth.

'I feel sorry for whoever has to snog her,' I said.

'Oh, wow. Look at these,' said Lucy, pulling me over to look at the racks displaying jewellery. Most of it was made out of transparent Perspex plasticky stuff. Chokers and gauntlets, with metal studs and spikes. 'I've seen this stuff. It glows in the dark in clubs.'

'Cool. And definitely different,' I said. 'Cressida may say it's all happening in Notting Hill, but this takes some beating.'

'Yeah, it's like galaxy princess meets Olive Oyle,' said Lucy as an assistant wearing a tiny black dress and striped tights walked past in knee-high lace-up boots with four-inch rubber soles.

'New rock,' said Ben, appearing behind us and pointing at the boots. 'Everyone's wearing them.'

Even Ben had made some concession to the style of the place. He'd replaced his usual John Lennon glasses with silver goggles and wore white overalls and silver space boots.

'Where's Iz?' asked Lucy.

'Getting changed.'

At that moment Izzie appeared at the end of the aisle.

'Like it?' she asked, looking shyly at Ben.

She looked *amazing*. Transformed.

She had on a short black dress with no sleeves and a scoop neck, but the skirt was extraordinary. It stuck out, as if someone had lined the hem with coat hanger wire. Like crinoline skirts from ages gone by. On her legs she wore a pair of the furry leggings like the assistant was wearing, only Izzie's were blue. On her arms she had a pair of turquoise gauntlets and round her neck a turquoise choker with metal spikes.

'You look like an alien rock singer,' I said.

'Rock chickerama,' said Lucy.

'I thought I'd get some electric blue eyelashes,' said Izzie. 'And maybe some blue hair extensions, you know, the ones that look like dreadlocks. What do you think, Lucy?'

Lucy's eyes were shining. 'I think,' she said, 'that this place is the biz boz. I mean, why look like your mum when you can look like an alien borg babe? This stuff is trekkie heaven.'

Nesta's Diary

Dear Diary

Had an awful day. I went gambling and lost all my money. Then I went to Camden with the girls and saw a million things I wanted but couldn't afford. I couldn't even buy a cappuccino and felt very miserable. Ben bought me one and I was very glad that Izzie didn't let on to him about me being a hopeless gambler drowning in materialism.

Although I wouldn't mind drowning in it a bit.

I think I have learnt a BIG lesson today. If I hadn't lost all that money I could have had a really nice time at Camden. I could have had Thai noodles and roasted nuts and even bought one of the galaxy princess chokers that are out-of-this-world fab.

I tried not to let on but actually I was v. fed up.

Chapter 11

Mobile Sloanes

The hall where the gig was to be held looked like a boy scout's hut. There was a tatty plywood stage at one end, battered plastic tables and chairs lining the walls and threadbare curtains at windows that looked like they hadn't been cleaned in a decade.

'Good turn-out,' said Lucy, looking round at the people gathered. There were to be three bands on and it looked like everyone had brought friends and family along for support.

'I can't wait to see Cressida's face when she sees this joint,' I said.

'Shabby chic is not a look to be sniffed at,' said Lucy. 'It can take years to perfect.'

A few moments later, I saw Simon appear at the back door with the Portobello Princesses. Predictably Cressida's face fell.

'Oh, here's WC,' said Lucy. 'Looks like she has a bad smell under her nose.'

'What else is new?' I said. 'Oh *do* let me introduce you properly.'

Simon was as sweet as Cressida was sour. Immediately after the introductions, he asked who wanted what to drink and went off to the bar in the adjoining pub. I went with him to use the ladies'.

I fixed my lipstick, then went into a cubicle and, not long after, I heard the door open and footsteps.

'What a dive,' said a voice I recognised. It was Cressida. 'And *erlack*, this place stinks. I would never have come if Tony wasn't going to be here.'

'So does this interest in him mean that you've finally got over Simon?' Tanya's voice.

Very slowly and quietly, I lifted my feet up in case either of them decided to check under the cubicle doors. I wanted to hear what they had to say.

'Oh, yah. Though one can't see why he's going out with the zebra.'

'The zebra?' asked Tanya.

'Nesta. Half black, half white,' sniggered Cressida.

Inside my cubicle, I gasped.

'That's *really* mean,' said Tanya. 'You're jealous because she's stunning and Simon fancies her and not you.'

You tell her, Tanya, I thought. I was tempted to yell out, 'Earth is full. Go home!' But I bit my tongue. I wanted to hear what else they had to say.

'Nah. He doesn't fancy her, not *really*. He's only doing it to be different,' said Cressida. 'He's far too good for her. He probably wants to upset your parents. Going out with a middle-class mixed-race girl is his way of rebelling. It's a phase.'

Agghhh. I thought. *Aaaghhhh*.

Tanya was silent for a moment. 'You know what, Cressida? You can be a total bitch sometimes.'

'You say that as if it's a bad thing,' laughed Cressida.

I heard someone open the door then slam it behind them. Tanya, I presume.

Then I heard some rustling and the hiss of a spray, then a scent of vanilla. I heard the door open and close again. Then it was quiet.

I waited a few seconds before lowering my feet back on to the floor. It felt like someone had hit me in the stomach and I bent over in pain. I *wished* I hadn't heard.

It couldn't be true, could it? Simon was only going out with me because I was like, a *novelty*? He wanted to appear *different*? My eyes pricked with tears. I thought Simon really liked me. And his mum seeemed very nice when I met her the other day. She hadn't seemed unduly upset, but had she just been acting polite and was secretly appalled?

It felt like someone had taken my breath away and I gasped for air. Then, suddenly, the flood gates opened and tears started running down my face.

Graffiti scrawled on the back of the loo door stared harshly back at me. 'Life's a bitch,' it said, 'and then you die.' Life *is* a bitch, I thought. My boyfriend's using me to upset his parents. My parents haven't got jobs. All I seem to do these days is want things I can't have. I've become really shallow. And I don't know anything any more.

Suddenly, there was a timid knock on the door.

'Are you all right in there?' It was Izzie's voice.

I unlocked the door. 'It's *me*,' I sobbed.

'Oh, Nesta,' she cried, pushing the door open properly. 'What's the matter?'

I took great gulps of air and tried to get out what I'd overheard. Izzie listened quietly but by the time I'd finished she looked angry.

'What a *cow*,' she said. She handed me a bit of loo paper and put her arm round me. 'I'd like to sock her in her stupid snotty face. I saw them just now, standing at the back of the room like, so superior. Like they're so above the rest of us.'

'Tanya's OK,' I said. 'She stuck up for me.'

'Then I don't know why she hangs round with Cressida. She should dump her. And have you seen them? It's like they're both stuck to their mobiles. They haven't had them off their ears since they arrived.'

'They're always like that,' I said.

'We should call them Mobile Sloanes,' said Izzie, smiling wickedly. 'I might even write a song about them. Mobile Sloanes. Ice-blonde clones . . . Yeah, I'll work on it.'

I was beginning to feel a bit better.

'Mobile Sloanes,' I laughed and blew my nose. Then, for the first time, I noticed what Izzie was wearing. She had on the gear from Cyberdog but she'd done her make-up bright silver with electric blue eyelashes and glittery blue nail polish. Her hair was gelled back into a high ponytail and she had a blue lightning symbol painted on her forehead like a cosmic third eye.

'Wow, Izzie, you look totally amazing.'

'You think? Not too much?'

'Yeah, *yeah*, too much. That's why it's so *cool*. You look *really* beautiful. Like a galaxy princess. I feel so boring beside you.'

'You look great, as well,' said Izzie. 'That biker-babe look really suits you.' I'd worn my old favourites – black leather trousers and jacket. 'You look a ton better than those two sloane clones out there. At least you have your own style.'

She gave me a hug and looked at me seriously. 'You mustn't let WC upset you. She's not worth it. You've been acting really oddly ever since you met her. Like you have to prove something. And, believe me, you don't, not to people like her. Me and Lucy have been really worried. It's not like you. So, come on, splash your face and let's get out of here.'

I did as I was told and reapplied my make-up, most of which had run down my face.

'We'll do a deal,' said Izzie, applying some bright blue lipstick. 'You go out there and show them how to have a good time. Get out on the floor and dance. And I'll get up on stage and show them just how cool us Norf London girls can be.'

'Deal,' I said and we shook hands. 'How are you feeling?'

Izzie stood up straight and put her shoulders back. Then she sank forward and leant against the wall. 'I'm terrified, Nesta. Absolutely terrified.'

Then she got out a little bottle of something and swigged it back.

'*Izzie?* You turning to drink?'

'It's larch,' she said. 'A Bach flower remedy for confidence.'

I love Izzie, I thought. Mad witch that she is.

As we went back into the hall, we saw that the first band had started up. Izzie disappeared backstage, so I went to join Lucy, who was talking to Simon.

'Is everything all right?' asked Simon, scrutinising me.

'Yeah, cool,' I said, then pulled him aside for a minute. 'I have to ask you something.'

'Looks serious,' he said. 'Shoot.'

'Are you going out with me to upset your parents?'

Simon looked horrified. 'Course not. Mum really liked you when you met her the other day. Why should it upset them?'

'With me being, you know . . .'

'What? Being *what*?' he asked, then he stopped and looked at me closely. 'Oh, I get it. Well actually, if I'm totally honest, I think Mum may be a bit upset. In fact, probably a lot . . . And so will Dad be when he meets you . . .'

Oh *no*, I thought. Cressida was right.

'See, Dad's going to be *insanely* jealous,' continued Simon, 'that I'm going out with the best-looking girl in London and he's far too old to get a look-in. And Mum, for the same reason. Jealous. You're naturally gorgeous and no matter how many facials or make-overs she has, she'll never look as good as you.'

He wrapped me in his arms and gave me a huge bear hug. 'OK?'

'OK,' I said. I could see Cressida out of the corner of my eye, looking daggers at me. Then she spotted Tony who had just walked in and was making a bee-line for Lucy.

She came over and hovered near us, hoping Tony'd notice her, but he only had eyes for Lucy.

I almost felt sorry for her as she desperately tried to get his attention and failed. She was standing all on her own. It was clear that Tanya wasn't speaking to her either, as she stood a distance away with her back turned.

After a while, Tony and Lucy went on to the dance floor to dance and Cressida came over.

'Who's that girl all over Tony?' she asked.

'That *girl* is Lucy,' I replied. 'One of my best friends. I introduced you earlier. And if you look closely you'll see that she's not all over him. In fact, it's the other way round.'

'I seriously doubt *that*,' said Cressida. 'She looks like she's hardly out of kindergarten.'

'Like Tony, do you?' I asked innocently.

'He's OK,' she said, looking round. 'Does he ever say anything about me?'

'You're *kidding*?' I said. 'He hasn't stopped talking about you since he met you.' It was true. He hadn't stopped going on about how stuck-up he thought she was. I could see Cressida was dying to ask me more, but at that moment Tanya waved at me and indicated to meet her outside.

I followed her out into the alleyway down the side of the pub. She had a huge Mulberry bag with her out of which she drew a bottle of champagne, a carton of orange and some plastic cups.

'Supplies,' she grinned. 'I brought it for me and Cress but, well, she's a pain and I thought you might like some. Ever had a Bellini?'

'No. What is it?'

'Champagne and orange juice. Actually it should be peach juice but they didn't have any at the offy. Want one?'

'Sure,' I said. I'd only ever had sips of wine before and I hadn't liked it at all. It was like drinking vinegar. But I didn't want to say no to Tanya when she was clearly making an effort to be friendly. And she *had* stood up for me before in the ladies'. A few sips would probably be OK, I decided. Specially if diluted with orange.

Tanya poured a beaker and handed it to me, then poured another for herself.

'To new friendships,' she said, as we slammed plastic cups and drank. Actually it was nice. Much better than the sour-ink taste of wine. The orange juice made it sweet and the champagne made nice bubbles that went up my nose.

'Want another?' asked Tanya.

I was beginning to feel game for anything. 'Go on,' I said and knocked back the second one.

A lovely giggly feeling came over me. I felt like the

champagne, all bubbly and light.

'Iz will be on soon,' I said. 'We'd better go back in.'

'Right,' said Tanya, slugging back her drink. 'Lessgo.'

On the way back into the hall, I felt giddy and giggly.

'Amazing,' I said to Tanya as we walked back into the hall with linked arms. 'Life can go up and down all in the space of half an hour. From misery to fun.'

Tanya hiccupped. 'Yah. Know watchya mean. Shit to champagne kindathing.'

King Noz had just started up their set so I went to join Simon and Tony where they were standing at the back of the hall.

'Where's Lucy?' I asked.

'Gone to check on Izzie, I think,' said Tony.

Lucy reappeared a few minutes later. She came straight over to me. 'Izzie told me what WC said about you. Honestly, what a cow.'

'A cow who's after Tony.' I said, then giggled. 'She's a cow and I'm a zebra. I told her that Tone fancied you and she was like, er, I doubt it. Like, not when he could have me.'

'Oh, *really*,' said Lucy, looking over at Cressida. 'OK. Just watch this, then.'

Lucy walked over to Tony, who was talking to Cressida again. She was doing the flick-flicky thing with her hair and looking deeply into his eyes. Tony, on the other hand, looked like he wanted to escape. Lucy went over and slipped her hand in his and his face lit up like a Christmas tree.

'Want to dance?' she asked as King Noz started playing a slow number. Tony nodded happily and went on to the floor with her. She snuggled into him, put her arms round his neck and whispered something in his ear. He replied by giving her a huge smoochy snog. It went on and *on*. A real Oscar-winner.

Cressida's jaw dropped open.

'What was that you were saying about seriously doubting that Tony fancied my friend?' I said casually.

Cressida turned on her heel and stomped over to Simon.

He looked over at me apologetically as she hauled him out on to the dance floor. Tanya came to stand next to me and when she saw no one was looking, she slipped me another beaker of Bellini.

'Thanks,' I said and knocked it back before anyone noticed.

Tee hee, I thought. It felt really good to be bad.

I watched Simon and Cressida on the dance floor. Neither of them were very good dancers. Simon was doing his best, which was a bit jerky, but Cressida – she was awful. She had no sense of rhythm at all.

'Immobile Sloane,' I said to Tanya, who looked at me quizzically.

'Mobile Sloanes,' I slurred, then remembered it had been Izzie who'd coined the phrase, not Tanya. Everything was a bit blurry.

'I mean Porobello Prin . . . princess. Thassit. Pincesses.'

'Are you OK?' asked Tanya.

'Never been better,' I said. 'Wanna dance?'

If there was one thing I could do well, it was dance. I'd show these Mobile Sloanes how it was done, I thought.

After the band finished the slow number, I saw Ben go and take the microphone.

'And now, ladies and gents, I'd like to introduce a new member of the band singing with us tonight for the first time. I'd like to introduce you all to the very lovely Miss Izzie Foster.'

He stood back to applaud as Izzie walked onstage. She looked fabulous and I cheered loudly along with everyone else. I felt so proud of her. S'my pal, I thought. Myverybestpal. Then the band started up and Izzie began to sing. Ben joined in with her for the choruses. They sounded wonderful. Really really great harmonies.

But no one was dancing.

People *oughta* be dancin', I thought. Makes the band look berra for the recor' company people. S'really important.

I decided *I'd* start them off. I'd do it for Izzie.

I made my way on to the dance floor, took off my

shoes and began to sway in time to the music. My head felt like it was spinning a bit, but if I listened closely to the beat, I could flow with it. I felt so light on my feet.

After a while, I noticed that everyone was watching me. It was my moment in the spotlight so I really went for it. Spinning. Hopping. Moving with the grooving. I was a diva. Dancing. Diva dancing. Yeah.

Then I noticed Izzie up on the stage. She was still singing but she was looking at me kind of strange.

Then I noticed Lucy. She was looking at me, kind of *mad*.

She walked on to the dance floor and hissed at me. 'Nesta. Go and sit down.'

'Why? Tryin' to gereveryone dancin . . .' I slurred.

'Everyone's *looking* at you,' said Lucy.

'S'all right,' I said, 'Un showin en how isdone.'

'It's *Izzie*'s moment,' whispered Lucy urgently. 'Not yours.'

She grabbed my wrist firmly and pulled me to the side of the dance floor.

'Woz happening?' I said. Everything seemed blurred and my mouth felt dry. I had a sudden urge to crawl under the table and fall asleep. 'Whezevybudy?'

'What's the matter with you?' asked Lucy.

'Ballooni,' I said. 'Snice. Tanyanme. Owange juice and champy-ain.'

'Oh *no*,' said Lucy. 'You're *drunk*. Wait here. I'll get Tony.'

I leant on my arm for a while and I must have dropped off as the next thing I knew Tony was nudging me. 'Time to go home, kiddo.' I looked over at the stage. King Noz were no longer playing.

I felt dreadful. I looked over to see where the others were and I could see Izzie, Ben and Lucy standing in the corner. They had their backs turned to me.

'Oops . . .' I thought as I remembered Izzie's face up on the stage.

Tony helped me to my feet. 'Come on, let's get some fresh air.'

'Where's Simon?' I asked as Tony put his arm round me and hauled me out to the pavement in front of the pub.

'Last time I saw him, he was desperately pouring water down Tanya's throat in an attempt to sober her up before their mum sees her and he gets the blame.'

'Oh dear,' I said. 'We had Balloonees. Sorrysorry.'

The cool night air woke me up a little and my head began pounding. A sudden thought made me panic. 'Is our mum here?'

Tony shook his head. 'No. She phoned to say Mrs Lovering is coming to get us.'

'Oh *no*,' I groaned. 'It will make Cressida's night to see us all getting in that old jalopy of theirs.'

'What does it matter what she thinks?' said Tony as a brand-new black Mercedes drove by and stopped a hundred metres past the pub.

A short distance behind it, at the traffic lights, I could see Lucy's mum's Beetle. I swear it was glowing in the dark like a giant turquoise insect. Oops! I thought. Those balloonees really *were* strong.

At that moment, Izzie came out and turned away when she saw me. She was followed by Lucy.

'Sorry, sorry . . .' I began.

'Tonight wasn't meant to be about you, Nesta,' said Lucy, turning on me. 'It was Izzie's big night, but somehow you managed to get all the attention as usual.'

As *usual*? Suddenly I felt like I wanted to sit on the pavement and cry. It *wasn't fair*. It *wasn't* my fault I'd drank the Balloonees. I was only trying to be friendly to Tanya who had stood up for me when WC had called me a zebra. *Then* she said Simon was too good for me.

I looked up the road at the dilapidated old banger approaching, then I looked at Cressida who was walking towards the black Mercedes with her nose in the air.

It was all too much.

I wanted to cry.

I wanted Simon.

But he only liked me when I was fun, *didn't* he?

He was always saying how much he liked my attitude. My winning attitude.

He liked Fun Nesta. All Singing, All Dancing Nesta. He wouldn't like All Crying Nesta, so I couldn't let him see me *now*.

Tears were queuing up at the back of my eyes. I could feel them. I had to get away.

'Tell Tony I've made my own way home, will you?' I called to Lucy, who was standing with her arm around Izzie.

And with that I ran off towards the tube station as fast as I could.

Chapter 12

%*@:-((Hungover)

The next morning, when I woke up, I felt like someone had glued my eyelids shut in the night. Heavy, ukky. Finally I pulled them open and turned over to look at the clock by my bed.

Eleven thirty. I groaned as the room began to spin and I remembered The Night Before. Pants, I thought. Oh, *pants*.

How did I get home?

And *who's* Riverdancing on my brain?

I could remember running away. I'd got round the corner away from the pub and stood by a brick wall to catch my breath. I remember that. I felt dreadful. All mixed up. I felt sick and I had to get home. Wanted Mum.

In the distance I could see a taxi with its light on. I was about to stick my hand out, when I remembered I hadn't enough money. I'd spent it on stupid scratchcards and couldn't be sure that anyone was home to pick up the fare.

I looked in my purse. A pound coin, three twenty pences and one five pence. Enough to get the tube at least.

I quickly made my way over to the tube station and past three dishevelled men swigging back cans of beer in a doorway. They stared at me as I hurried past.

'Wanna play out, little girl?' laughed one of them.

I kept my head down. This was the first time I'd been out so late on my own and I tried to remember what Miss Watkins had told us at school about travelling alone at night. That was it. Walk confidently and don't make eye contact with anyone.

As I reached the tube entrance, I almost fell over a huddle by the ticket office. It was a boy all wrapped up in a sleeping bag. He couldn't have been much older than me. In front of him was a handwritten sign saying, 'Hungry and Homeless. Can you help?' Next to him was a black dog. The two of them appeared so pathetic, as they looked up at me hopefully.

I went and got my ticket then put the rest of my change in the boy's can.

'Sorry,' I blurted. 'S'all I got.'

Then I made my way down to the platform. Luckily, I didn't have to wait long for a train. Remembering rule two, don't get into an empty carriage, I made for the centre of the train, which was full of people. I sat down and stared at the floor.

Some lads were sitting a couple of seats away. They were stuffing down hamburgers and the smell of onions and ketchup was inescapable. I felt like I was going to throw up.

'Wanna bite of my hot dog?' called one. All his friends started sniggering.

I kept looking at the floor. I wanted to cry. I wanted my mum.

I was out like a shot when we reached Highgate and I ran up the stairs and out into the lane outside the station. It was so dark. Black. Shadowy. What had *possessed* me to make my own way home? As I ran along the lane, I felt really frightened.

I manoeuvred my bag so that it was over my shoulder diagonally. (Third rule of travelling alone, as it's hard to snatch a bag from that position.) Then I found my house keys and put them in my jacket pocket (fourth rule, so that if your bag is snatched, at least you can get in your front door). Miss Watkins would be pleased I'd managed to remember so much of her lesson.

Then I legged it as fast as I could.

Everywhere looked menacing. The trees, cars going by, people in the street, they all looked shifty. My heart was thumping in my chest as I hurtled along the street and into our road and up the steps to our flat. I fumbled with the locks, then, at last, the welcome sight of house lights, the sound of the TV.

I was home.

Dad came out of the living-room. 'Nesta,' he said.

'Dad,' I said. 'Brilliant.'

Then I threw up all over the hall.

Ah yes, it was all coming back to me as I lay under the duvet. I wondered how long I could stay there hiding. Somehow, I didn't want to go downstairs. What a mess. Was there a way to turn back the clock? I wondered. Twenty-four hours? A week?

Everyone was mad with me. Dad. Tony. Lucy. Izzie.

And myself.

I looked around my bedroom and remembered the face of the homeless boy in the tube station. His eyes were so empty. He had nothing and I had everything. CDs, books, clothes, perfume, make-up, a computer, my own TV, a mobile – but most of all a home. A safe place to return to.

And what had I done for the last few weeks?

Think about myself non-stop and all the things I hadn't got. All of it stuff I didn't even really need. And where had it got me? Nowhere.

I had never felt so miserable in all my life. Izzie was right with her Ben the Buddhist stuff. Desire makes you miserable.

I won't give in to another desire as long as I live.

I winced when I thought about Izzie. I'd *ruined* her big special night. She'd looked so beautiful and had been so brave getting up there, facing her private fear and singing and . . .

I started crying again.

I am the most *horrid* person that ever lived, I thought. *Bad. Selfiiiiiish. Self-obsesseeeed.* And *God . . . starv . . . ing*!!

The aroma of frying bacon was wafting up the stairs.

Feed me. Feed me *now*! My film for the day was the *Little Shop of Horrors* and my role was that ever-hungry alien plant that demands food. Images of toast, coffee, muffins and peanut butter sailed in front of my eyes.

My stomach was growling and all further thoughts of contrition disappeared as I tried to think of a way of sneaking into the kitchen before the inevitable confrontation with Those Who Shall Be Obeyed. Parents.

I slipped into my dressing-gown and made my way into the kitchen. Mum, Dad and Tony were sitting like High Court judges on stools at the breakfast bar, staring at me as I crept in. No getting out of this, I thought.

'Er, morning,' I said as I tried to gauge the atmosphere. Something was going on, as Mum and Dad looked surprisingly cheerful considering that I'd done the technicolour yawn all over the hall the previous night. There was a bottle of what looked remarkably like champagne in an ice bucket. And a carton of orange juice! In front of Mum and Dad were two crystal glasses.

I went and sniffed a glass and the smell made me retch as it brought back last night.

'Are you drinking Balloonis?' I demanded.

'No, Buck's Fizz,' said Mum.

'Erlack, how *could* you? You'll get an awful headache, you know!'

Dad laughed. 'Actually, the word is Bellini. It's champagne with peach juice – Buck's Fizz is with orange.'

'Whatever,' I said. 'But first thing in the *morning*? Gross.'

'And good morning to you, sunshine,' said Dad.

'Actually, we're celebrating,' said Mum. 'I would have told you last night but you'd already gone to bed by the time I was back. See the reason I couldn't pick you up last night was because I was having dinner with the studio boss and . . .'

'And?' I asked.

'*And* my contract has been renewed for another three years,' grinned Mum. 'Plus, they've given me a rise.'

I went over and gave her a hug. 'That's brilliant, Mum! Well done. So does that mean that everything's going to be all right?'

'For a while,' said Dad, raising his glass. 'Life goes on.'

Tony hadn't said a word through all this. He was eating a bacon toastie and glowering at me through slit eyes.

Finally he couldn't hold it in any longer. 'What the *hell* did you think you were doing going off on your own last night? Me and Simon spent ages looking for you up and down Kentish Town Road. Anything could have happened . . .'

Oh God. *Simon*. I hadn't even said goodbye to him. Might as well add his name to the ever-growing list of people who were mad with me.

'I got the tube home,' I said, eyeing up the pile of toast on the bar.

'Well *we* didn't know that. You said to Lucy that you were making your own way home. You weren't answering your mobile. *We* didn't know whether you'd tried to walk or get a bus or what . . .'

Mum and Dad nodded along with Tony. It was like he was the strict parent, not them.

'It was far too late for someone of your age to be out on your own,' continued Tony. 'There are some real nutters on the streets.'

I decided not to argue. 'Sorry,' I muttered and I reached out for a piece of toast.

'Sore head?' asked Dad.

I nodded. 'Tanya gave me one of those things you're drinking. I didn't realise they were so strong.'

'How many did you have?'

'Er . . . three. And *never again*, I double promise,' I said, turning to Tony. 'Did Lucy or Izzie say anything? Are they speaking to me?'

'Dunno,' said Tony. 'They went home with Lucy's mum while Simon and I looked for you. You really don't think, do you? That people might be worried.'

'Bet Lucy and Izzie weren't worried.'

'Yeah. They did seem kind of mad,' said Tony. 'Specially Lucy.'

I poured a cup of coffee from the cafetière.

'I'll text message them right away,' I said.

'Chicken. Why don't you ring or go round?' asked Tony. 'I think you owe them a face-to-face apology.'

I couldn't. Not yet. I knew I couldn't face them being mad, not today.

Later that afternoon, Dad came and tapped on my bedroom door.

I was still feeling icky and my head hurt, so I'd gone for a lie-down. He came in and sat at the end of the bed.

'How's my princess?'

'Not great,' I said. 'Feels like a family of goblins in hobnailed boots are jumping about in my head.'

'Do you want anything?'

'No.' I still wasn't sure if I was going to get more of a telling-off so I decided that, if there was one coming, it was best to get it over with. 'Aren't you mad with me?'

Dad shook his head. 'No, not mad, Nesta.' Then he grinned. 'Tony gave you enough of a roasting at breakfast. And I think you learnt your lesson as far as drink goes.'

'First and last,' I said.

'I doubt it,' said Dad. 'But maybe wait until you're a bit older before you go knocking back half a bottle of champagne, even if it *is* diluted with orange. Lesson one about drink – champagne gives a killer hangover to even the most hardy of drinkers. So lesson learnt. No, I'm not mad at you. More concerned than anything. Mum says you've been a bit down lately. And you sure looked bad last night.'

Dad was looking at me with such kindness that I felt tears well up in my eyes. His reaction was so unexpected. I thought I was in for a major grounding. Suddenly it all came pouring out and I told him all about the journey home and how scared I was and . . .

'. . . and I've got this new boyfriend. But I think he only likes me because I'm a laugh. And sometimes I don't *feel* like being a laugh. It's exhausting, being the entertainment *all* the time . . .'

'So be yourself,' said Dad. 'If he's worth it he'll stick around for the highs *and* the lows. Everyone has days when they feel a bit blue. It's OK. It's called being human. And if you're going to have a relationship with someone, it's important to feel comfortable enough to be real with them. Have you let this boy know how you feel?'

I shook my head. 'No. He's going to Courchevel soon. Skiing. And there was a spare place and he asked if I wanted to go . . . Oh, Dad, it's been *awful*. He's really rich and I haven't been able to keep up.'

'It sounds to me like you and he have some talking to do. Tell him who you are. How you feel. And if he stays around, great. If he doesn't, he wasn't worth it.'

He got up and walked over to my desk in the corner. I thought he was going to say something else, but he'd spotted the paper with the model agency ad circled. Oh *no*, I thought, don't let him look at that. Too late. He sat down at my desk chair and read the ad.

I put my head under the pillow.

'Oh, Nesta,' he said. 'You haven't contacted these people, have you?'

I nodded my head under the pillow.

'Did they ask for money?' he asked slowly.

I gave a small nod.

'Come out of there,' he said. 'I'll tell you something about these agencies. They make their money by exploiting young girls like you. Believe me, I know. I've worked with model agencies for over two decades and the good ones won't ask you for money for registration or a portfolio. The good ones will see it as an investment in your future. These other places tell all sorts of kids they've got potential, but only to get their money out of them. They never get you real work.'

'Sorry . . .' I whispered.

'Look, if modelling is so important to you, we'll look into it when you're sixteen.'

'But I don't want to be a model,' I said. 'I want to be an actress.'

'So what's with the ad in the paper?'

'I wanted to earn some money. To help you and Mum out . . . And buy some clothes and stuff.'

Dad laughed. 'Oh, Nesta. You don't have to worry about us yet. Maybe when we're old and dribbling but . . .'

'But you haven't got a film to work on, have you?'

'There are a few possibilities around. I just don't want to take the first thing that comes along,' said Dad. 'Plus, I'd like to work closer to home for a while, keep an eye on my wayward daughter. We'll see. Nothing is ever certain in the film industry and if you want to be an actress, you'd better get used to that fact. Actors, like directors, aren't always in work and you're only ever as good as your last job. There's an awful lot of talent out there that is, as we say, "resting" or in between jobs.'

'You mean unemployed?'

'Exactly.'

'I hope something comes up for you, Dad.'

'It will. It always has up until now,' he smiled, 'and in the meantime, there's a certain young man I think you ought to talk to.'

After Dad had gone, I dialled Simon's mobile number. The answering service was on.

I tried his home number.

'He's gone down to Wiltshire,' said a voice I didn't recognise.

Course. I'd forgotten. He'd told me on the night of the gig that he was going down to the country house for a few days.

I decided I'd send him an e-mail.

Hi Simon,

I'm writing this to you to say goodbye for ever.

Also to apologise for last night. Tony told me that you were looking for me. I am sorry if you were worried, but I got home safe then threw up all over the hall. Mum and Dad were really chilled about it.

I can't come to Courchevel. My family isn't as rich as yours and at the moment we can't afford extras like skiing trips.

That's why I think it's best if we say goodbye. I can't keep up with all the things you do, like skiing and horse-riding. Not on the pocket money I get.

And not being able to keep up makes me miserable. Talking of which, I do. Get miserable sometimes, that is. In fact, some days I can be grumpy and horrid. Downright repugnant. In the weeks I've known you, I don't think you have seen the real me. You said you liked me because I was so confident and funny. Well now you know the truth. I'm not like that all the time.

Sorry about everything. And maybe we can still text message sometimes.

Lots of love and, as Ali G says, keep it real.

Nesta.

Before I could change my mind, I pressed 'Send' and off it went.

Nesta's Diary

After breakfast, I sent both Izzie and Lucy the same message:
RUStlFrnds?

No reply

So I sent:
%*@: -(hungover
:-[unhappy
SrySrySry

No reply

So *then* I sent:
:-C   really unhappy
:-/   confused
:"-(crying
IluvU
SrySrySry

No reply.

E-mailed Simon to say goodbye. Kind of hoped that he'd do something extraordinary like abseil down the side of our flat with a box of Black Magic and declare his undying love and say that he'll never let me go. Or stand outside my window with a guitar singing a love song.

But no such luck.

No reply from Simon. No reply from Lucy or Izzie.

So that's it. No girlfriends. No boyfriend.

My life is over.

Chapter 13

SrySrySry

'For heaven's sake, go round,' said Mum after two days of me moping about the flat. 'When does term start again? I can't wait. *Go*. Apologise. Make up.'

'I will,' I said. 'I was just hoping that, well, they might have replied to one of my text messages or something.'

'And what about Simon? Any word from him?'

I shook my head. 'No. I don't expect I'll ever hear from him again either.'

'But I thought you liked him?

'I did. I *do*. But . . . I don't think he'd like me if he really knew me.'

'Have you given him a chance?'

'Sort of. I was really honest in my e-mail. But he hasn't replied. Nobody likes me any more.'

Mum came and gave me a big hug. 'I do,' she said. 'In fact, I love you. Now, go on, phone your friends.'

I took a deep breath and went to the phone. I dialled Izzie's number first.

'She's gone to Camden Lock with Lucy,' said Mrs Foster.

'Thanks,' I said and put down the phone. Out having fun without me. It was too much. I couldn't let it go on.

'Mum. They're at the Lock,' I called from the hall. 'I'm going to look for them.'

'Good for you,' said Mum, getting her purse. 'And here's a little spending money. Get yourself something you like while you're down there.'

Twenty quid! I gave Mum a hug. Happiness is some dosh in your pocket and permission to spend, I thought, as I set off for the tube.

As usual, the Lock was heaving with people. I decided to try Cyberdog first as Izzie and Lucy might be visiting Ben.

'Ben? Nah, he's not in today,' said one of the alien mutants who worked there.

I had a quick look round to see if the girls were there anyway, but there was no sign of them. May as well have a quick look at the clothes while I'm here, I thought, as I saw the rails of clothes and jewellery. On display there was a choker like the one Ben had borrowed for Izzie. Transparent turquoise with studs on it. I tried it on and it looked stunning. Then a little voice in my head said, buy it for Izzie. That's it! I realised. I'll use the money from Mum to buy something for Iz and Lucy. Then, if I don't find them, I'll go round and beg forgiveness.

I quickly bought the choker for Izzie, then went to look for something for Lucy. I wasn't sure Cyberdog was her style so I went to look at some of the stalls in the main courtyard. There were some brilliant T-shirts for sale. I flicked through the rails trying to decide which one Lucy might like.

One said, 'If you think I'm a bitch, wait until you meet my mother'.

Another, 'www.whassup.com'.

Another said, 'Mad Cow'. Probably not appropriate to give to a friend who I'm trying to make up with, I thought. Nor was the next one. That said, 'I hate everyone and you're next'.

Then I saw one that was perfect for Lucy. It had two inky hands positioned right over the boobs. She has a hang-up about being flat-chested and this would make her laugh.

I paid the stall owner and made my way through the rest of the stalls. I spent over an hour looking everywhere for Lucy and Izzie but there was no sign. I looked in the indoor *and* outdoor market.

By the entrance to the indoor market was a stall selling T-shirts and a huge sign saying that you could make up your own slogan. Five pounds.

A current trend going round school was to have the name of an opponent or rival written on your chest. I could have Jennifer Lopez written on one for Izzie and Stella McCartney for Lucy. I looked in my purse, but didn't have enough left. Another time, I thought.

I had four pounds fifty left, so I went and bought an Easter egg instead, then took a deep breath and phoned Lucy's.

Her brother Steve answered. 'Er, is Lucy back yet?'

'Yeah,' he said. 'Just a . . .'

'No, no Steve, don't call her. Is Izzie there as well?'

'Yeah.'

'OK, don't tell them I called, OK?'

'OK.'

Half an hour later, I rang the doorbell at Lucy's house and Steve let me in. 'They're in the bedroom,' he said.

'Thanks,' I said and crept up the stairs.

Should I knock or just burst in? I stood at the top of the stairs wondering what was the best plan of action. Maybe I should listen at the door for a moment? No. Bad idea, I thought. Last time I eavesdropped I heard Cressida calling me a zebra. No, there was only one way forward. I must think of a character from a film that I can be. Someone who needs to grovel . . .

Got it! I thought, and got down on my knees. I opened the door and crawled in.

'I'm not worthy. I'm not worthy,' I said, prostrating myself at their feet. My film for today was *Wayne's World*. In it, Wayne and his mate Garth kneel and bow in front of their rock idol, Alice Cooper.

Lucy and Izzie looked very surprised to see me and exchanged looks.

'What on earth are you doing, Nesta?' asked Izzie.

Maybe she hasn't seen *Wayne's World*, I thought, as I got up off the floor. 'Er, throwing myself on your mercy,' I said. 'Admitting that I am the lowest of the low, an amoeba. The slime on an amoeba. The slime on the slime of an amoeba. Please guys. I miss you *so* much. And I know I blew it. And the way I behaved at the gig was unforgivable. I'm so sorry. Please be my friends again. I brought presents and everything . . .'

I handed them the choker, the T-shirt and the Easter egg.

'Please. Sorry,' I continued. 'Buddhists are into forgiveness, aren't they? Izzie. Huh? Guys? I know I am the worst friend in the whole world. Truly horrid and I *beg* you to have mercy on me and . . .'

Izzie and Lucy burst out laughing. 'We were just about to call you,' said Izzie. 'We miss you too.'

'And we know it wasn't all your fault,' said Lucy. 'You were upset after those things WC said about you. And then the champagne . . .'

'But that was such a show you just put on,' laughed Izzie. 'We couldn't *possibly* have interrupted.'

I sank on to the bed. Happy happy.

'And we have a pressie for you,' said Izzie, grinning wickedly. 'We were down the Lock and saw this T-shirt stall that does slogans.'

'I saw it,' I gasped. 'I was going to have some done but I'd run out of money . . .'

'Well we had one done for you,' said Izzie, pulling out a bag and handing it to me.

Lucy was grinning like a maniac.

I pulled out the T-shirt and burst out laughing when I saw what they'd had written on the front.

'Brilliant,' I said.

They'd had a name printed in a red heart.

CRESSIDA.

We spent a top afternoon catching up. So much had happened. Lucy's thinking about getting back with Tony, though she hasn't let on to him yet.

'Going to keep him guessing a bit longer,' she said.

'Serves him right,' I laughed. 'It's *usually* his motto, treat 'em mean to keep 'em keen.'

'Exactly,' grinned Lucy.

Izzie also had news. The talent scout had turned up to watch the bands and he'd liked what he heard.

'Early days,' she said. 'But he's asked us to send a demo CD in. Fingers crossed.'

'And what about you?' asked Lucy. 'You and Simon?'

'Over,' I said. 'It wasn't right. I haven't heard from him since the gig.'

'Oh, I am sorry,' said Izzie. 'I liked him.'

'So did I,' I said.

Later that afternoon, we all went down to watch a repeat of 'The O.C.'. It was a really good episode and I felt over the moon to be with my friends again.

About ten minutes into the programme, my mobile rang.

I leapt up and answered it. I put one hand over the receiver and pointed at the phone with the other. '*Simon . . .*' I whispered.

I went into the hall so I could have some privacy. If I was going to have to grovel, then I wanted to do it without an audience.

'Hey,' he said.

'Hey,' I replied, thinking I really must work on my conversation skills. I realised I was very nervous.

'I've just got your e-mail,' he said. 'I'm sorry I didn't get in touch sooner – I left my laptop and mobile at the London house. I did try and ring you from Wiltshire but your number's unlisted.'

'Yeah,' I said. Oh for God's sake, get a grip, Nesta, I thought. But I couldn't think of anything riveting to say.

'I've got a few things I want to tell you,' continued Simon, sounding very serious. 'Three things, in fact.'

Here we go, I thought. I'm going to be dumped.

I went and sat on the stairs.

'First. Sorry about my sister. I don't know what she was thinking about, giving you all that champagne. Second, even more sorry about Cressida. Tanya told me what she said about you. Apparently you'd overheard. Lucy told Tony and Tony told me. Very very sorry about that. Personally I'm never going to speak to her again and I think Tanya's dropping her as a friend as well. And thirdly, I'd like to keep seeing you even if you are horrid, grumpy and downright repugnant. I have days when I feel crap too. I agree that being real is all part of a relationship. Accepting the package, not just the good bits.'

'But what about . . . you know?' I said. 'Your world, my world.'

'No,' said Simon. 'It's *not* like that. There *is* no my world, your world. I'm so against that stuff.'

'Cressida didn't see it that way.'

'Just because we're from the same background doesn't mean we think the same way, Nesta. To think we do is as insulting as me thinking all Italians are the same. Or all Australians. Or all North Londoners. There's good and bad everywhere. Open- and narrow-minded. Generous and mean. It hasn't got anything to do with where someone grew up or what their mum or dad earns.'

I felt like I'd had another telling-off. Point taken, I thought, as the words of John Lennon's 'Imagine' popped into my head and I had to resist a sudden urge to sing.

'Cressida is a snobby pain and always has been,' continued Simon. 'That's why I finished with her in the first place. She doesn't get it. It's what's inside a person that counts. Whether they're nice or not. So . . .?'

'So?' I asked.

'Er. So, can I see you when I come back from skiing?'

'Mmm. I'll have to think carefully about everything you've said. I'll text you,' I said. 'Sometime.'

'Oh. OK,' he said, sounding very disappointed.

I waited thirty seconds after he'd hung up, then sent my message:

GetYaCoatUvePuld   CUL8R XXXXXXXXX (H) (H) (H)

He sent back:

☺ ☺ ☺ ☺ ☺ ☺ ☺ ☺ ☺ ☺ ☺ ☺ ☺ ☺ ☺ ☺ ☺ ☺ ☺ ☺

<3<3<3<3<3<3<3<3<3<3<3<3<3<3<3<3<3<3